Overboard

Elizabeth Fama

LAUREL-LEAF
BOOKS

For my husband, John,

and our children, Sally, Eric, Gene, and Lydia.

I love you.

Published by
Dell Laurel-Leaf
an imprint of
Random House Children's Books
a division of Random House, Inc.
New York

Visit us on the Web! www.randomhouse.com/teens

Educators and librarians, for a variety of teaching tools, visit us at
www.randomhouse.com/teachers

ISBN: 0-553-49436-8

Reprinted by arrangement with Cricket Books

Printed in the United States of America

February 2005

10 9 8 7 6 5 4 3 2 1

OPM

Emily might have been the only fourteen-year-old in the world who could change the sheets of a hospital bed with the patient still in it. She had done it more times than she cared to remember.

"I didn't come to help," Emily said, refusing the stack of folded sheets that her mother held out to her. "I just came to see if you and James would be home for dinner tonight." She glanced around the clinic. "Where's your loyal candy striper? Madjid is good at beds now."

"We don't use the term 'candy striper' here, Em. I wish you'd be polite to him, at least." Olivia wiped sweat from her forehead onto the sleeve of her white lab coat. "Anyway, Madjid's looking for a repairman to fix the air conditioner."

"What's the point? It never works," Emily griped. The humidity was stifling, as it always was in Indonesia, and today there was an odor in the clinic that pinched at the back of her nose and throat. She breathed through her mouth to dull the scent.

"Please, Emily . . . the bed? I'd really appreciate it . . ." Olivia said, holding up the sheets again. Emily took them from her with a sigh.

Olivia nodded toward a cot with a sleeping boy no more than five years old. "It's Yaso's bed, over there. Thanks, honey."

The boy's gown had fallen to the side, and Emily saw that his leg was in a cast up to the hip. Farther down the row of beds there was a dark, still little girl with an intravenous tube snaking from her arm up a pole to a plastic bag filled with clear fluid. She was glistening with sweat.

"Little Rabina's having a rough day," Olivia said over her shoulder. "Otherwise I'd do it."

Little Rabina, Emily grumbled to herself. Rabina didn't seem all that bad today. Olivia had been hovering over the seven-year-old for the past two weeks, ever since the girl's parents had brought her in with a ruptured appendix. The family was from a small village twenty miles south and they had allowed the *dukun*, the local healer, to use his folk potions and prayers to treat her, but she never got well. Emily's father, James, had saved Rabina's life with an emergency operation. Still, Emily thought, Rabina was being stubbornly slow about her recovery.

Emily went over to the cot that needed changing. When she got there she discovered the source of the odor in the clinic. The boy had relieved himself on the bed in his sleep, and his urine had the acrid smell of antibiotics.

His gown was soaked in the front. The sheets and pad were soaked beneath him.

"Great," she said with a huff. She put the sheets on a chair next to his cot and went to the nurses' station to get a new gown and a wet washcloth.

The trick to making a bed with the patient still in it is to make it one half at a time. Emily turned the little boy onto his right side and untucked the old sheet and pad, rolling them up against his back. Then she made half of the bed with the new sheet and pad, neatly rolling up the excess and laying it alongside the roll of dirty linens. Next she turned him onto his left side so that he was lying on the clean sheets, slid the dirty linens off the bed, unrolled the second half of the clean linens, and made the rest of the bed. Finally, after being turned twice, Yaso began to stir.

Emily eased him onto his back and straightened the damp gown in front, knowing that even the youngest patients could be modest. Yaso opened his eyes, so she tried to raise the head of the cot a notch or two, but the mechanism was stuck. She yanked it hard, and it slid into place with a jolt.

"You're very strong," Yaso said in his own language.

"Strong, like a bull." She wrinkled her nose at him and made a snorting noise.

Yaso laughed and tried to snort like a bull himself.

"You are good," she smiled.

"How old are you?" he asked.

"I am one hundred years old," she said, sitting in the chair with a sigh. Emily had found that Indonesians often asked personal questions, and it wasn't rude to give nonsensical, evasive answers.

"You speak Bahasa Indonesia well," the boy said.

"That is because I have lived here for too long."

"I know you. You're the doctors' daughter. You help in the clinic, like that boy, Madjid."

"Sometimes."

He looked into Emily's clear, green-gray eyes. "Ooh, your eyes! You have glass eyes!"

Emily shook her head "no" and handed him the washcloth. He accepted it, but continued to stare into her eyes.

Emily looked away. She bent down to escape his gaze, wrapped his old sheets into a ball, and put them on the floor next to her chair. Then she held up the new gown for him to see. He looked at it blankly, but was riveted back to her eyes.

"Please wash yourself and put this on," she said. She frowned, looking at his cast. "Will you need help washing and dressing?"

"I want to try by myself first," he said.

Emily said, "I will be here if you need me." She put the folded gown next to him on the bed and turned her chair away to give him privacy.

While she waited she reached out her long legs and pointed her toes in her sandals. She clasped her hands together, rounded her shoulders, and cracked her knuckles in front of her. Her underarms felt moist, and two wet marks stained her blouse, so she quickly brought her hands down onto her lap. She was wearing a long floral scarf around her head, a *kerudung*, and it itched in the heat, but it covered her blond hair and helped avoid endless conversation on that subject.

Emily was hungry, and it made her feel more hollow than ever. She looked down the row of cots at her mother, head bowed, eyes closed, listening through a stethoscope to the bony chest of Rabina. Olivia's blond hair slipped from behind her ears and fell in front of her face. Soon, Emily decided hazily, the stethoscope would become a permanent physical link between Olivia and Rabina, like an inorganic umbilical cord.

"I'm ready," the boy said. Emily turned her chair back. He had put the gown on but was unable to fasten the ties.

"You're so big!" he said, as she stood over him to reach his back.

"Yes, I know."

"And so white!"

She looked at her pale hands tying the back of the gown closed. The veins branched up from her knuckles to her wrists, like blue rivers.

Actually, I'm transparent, she thought with disgust.

"Yes," she said out loud, "very white."

2

The air conditioner was still broken, but Madjid had returned.

"Good afternoon, Ehm-i-lee," he said in English. "How are you today?"

He smiled with his eyebrows up, expectantly. His eyes were so black that Emily couldn't distinguish the pupils, and his thick eyelashes brushed against the lenses of his glasses. His teeth were white and straight and waiting, but Emily did not smile back. She hated it when he practiced English on her.

"Not well, thank you," she said. "Hot, oppressed, irritable."

His eyebrows fell. "Oh," he said, turning away. "I am sorry . . ."

Emily swept the clinic with a push broom. James was reading the medical chart of an infant in a crib. A large fly crawled undisturbed across his forehead.

"Do I have to stay here, James?" Emily whined.

There was a long pause. She knew her father had heard her. There was almost always a delay between her questions and his answers. His brain was like a computer running too many tasks at once, with each job queued in order of arrival. Or rather for him—an emergency surgeon by training—the jobs were sorted, like wounded soldiers, in order of urgency.

Emily bumped his feet with the broom.

"Override input buffer," she commanded the computer.

"Huh?" he said, looking up. She waited. The computer in his mind accessed her question and provided a response.

"Uh, you have to stay here in Banda Aceh, yes. But you don't have to stay here in the clinic if you'd rather go to the house."

Funny. Ha, ha, she thought.

James checked his watch and rubbed his eyes with his fingers, pushing his glasses up and onto his forehead. He readjusted the glasses.

"Olivia and I will be here late," he said. "Do you have homework you could do?" Before she could answer he looked back at his chart. "Or, don't you . . . want to help more?" he said haltingly. She could tell he was talking and reading at the same time. "The kids would like it if you stayed. Still . . . if you'd rather go home, or out with friends . . . that's fine, too."

"What do you mean, 'out with friends'?" Emily leaped on the phrase. "Just which friends did you have in mind?"

James held his breath for a second, looked up from the chart, and let out a sigh. "Em, don't let's get into this right here . . ." he began.

"Why not right here?" she challenged him. "I never see you anyplace else!" Her ears felt hot, and she knew if they hadn't been covered they would show red and ugly. The pitch of her voice rose. "So? How *do* you expect me to make friends when we *move* every two years?"

"You're going overboard again, Em," James said quietly.

"Overboard?" Her voice cracked. She gestured around her. "Look at this place! Why am I here? I know why you're here — to save the world. But I feel like a freak most of the time! Do you even care that I have no friends?"

"Whoa," James said, hugging the chart. "No one thinks you're a freak. . . . Everyone likes you —"

"I never asked to come here!" Emily interrupted. "I have nothing in common with anyone, and that's not going to change until we go home."

Across the room, Olivia left Rabina's bedside and strode toward her daughter with her eyebrows furrowed.

"Emily!" she hissed when she got close enough. "What do you think you're doing?"

"Nothing!" Emily said, looking away to avoid her mother's glare. She added sulkily, "I'm not doing anything but sweating in here."

"And disturbing everyone," Olivia said. "This isn't the place for a temper tantrum. We'll discuss your issues at home." She put an arm around Emily's waist and lowered her voice, "You *know* these kids are sick . . ."

Emily looked sheepishly around the ward. Rabina's parents had arrived. The mother was a beautiful, small woman wearing a flowing batik *sarung* skirt with a matching *selendang* — a breast-and-shoulder cloth. She clutched an unidentifiable, tattered stuffed animal to her chest. Her husband had his shirt buttoned all the way up to the neck, despite the heat. Madjid was standing at the nurses' station. He shook his head at Emily and turned back to his work.

The air was suddenly so moist and heavy that Emily couldn't breathe. She was such an idiot sometimes, she thought. A gangly, awkward idiot.

"I'm sorry," she whispered as she spun around and ran out. She was sorry she had made a fuss, but also sorry for herself that she was here at all — floating alone on Sumatra.

3

Emily fumbled as she tried to put her key in the lock. The rain trickled down her neck and made her shiver. She stepped in and closed the door, then walked toward the middle of the dark room, passing her hand slowly to the left and to the right in front of her, like a blind person in an unfamiliar place. The string from the light fixture snaked around her forearm. She yanked the string hard. "Would it be asking too much to have a switch near the door?" she said to no one.

The light was also a ceiling fan, and the sluggish breeze it created reminded her to open the windows—just a crack, because the rain poured down too steadily to open them wide.

She sank into the living room chair with a sigh. Her

stomach felt queasy now; she was so hungry and hot. For a moment her mind was blank. She closed her eyes, feeling wet and tired and heavy.

She imagined that she was dead in this position. Her parents would drag themselves through the door in the wee hours of the morning, empty-looking, with rings around their eyes from sitting at Rabina's bedside all night. They would say hello to the lifeless Emily, get themselves a bite to eat, and go to bed.

"Turn off the light when you go to sleep, please, Em," James would say to Emily's corpse over his shoulder.

" 'Night, honey," Olivia would add.

The cell phone rang, and Emily opened her eyes.

The house they had rented was simple, with just one bedroom for James and Olivia, a small kitchen, one bathroom, and a pullout sofa in a corner of the living room for Emily. The owners were an older couple who had never installed a phone; they had always lived very well without one, they said, and the telephone service was haphazard in this section of Aceh anyway. But Emily's parents needed the cell phone to keep in touch with the hospital.

Emily followed the ringing. She located the phone on her bed, under a pile of half-dirty clothes.

"*Selamat malam,*" she answered.

"What?" was the only reply. From that one word she knew it was her uncle.

"Hi, Matt!" she said.

With her free hand she began unwinding the scarf from her head.

"Oh, Squirt, is that you? I thought for a second I had dialed wrong."

"Where are you, Matt? On the ferry?"

"No, I'm on the island already, in Sabang. I've just registered in this lodge-thing your mom and dad told me about — Losmen Pulau Jaya. They're at the clinic?"

"Of course . . ." Emily finished unwrapping her *kerudung* and dropped the scarf on the floor. She scratched her scalp furiously with her fingertips.

"Work, work, work," Matt said. The connection crackled. There was a second of total silence and then the end of a sentence, ". . . ever do anything else?"

"Sorry, Matt, you're breaking up."

"Wait . . . is that better? Say, why don't you come tourist with me on Weh for a couple of days? There's a ferry tomorrow at noon. I could meet you when it arrives here."

Emily paused. She knew the island of Weh. She had been there for a day and a night once when neither of her parents was on call. Together they had found a deserted strip of beach on the rocky eastern coast. The sand was as white as ceiling paint. Emily remembered digging an enormous lagoon on the beach, with a canal leading to the sea. A homely, gray fish had wandered up her canal and become trapped in the lagoon. All afternoon James and Olivia had sat in folding chairs, wearing straw hats and reading novels, while Emily shored up her lagoon. She had stocked it with native plants, pieces of dead coral, and rocks. She had experimented with different foods for her fish tenant, but it never did eat anything. As the tide came in and overflowed her lagoon, the waves had eventually carried the fish to freedom.

Finally she said, "Did you ask James and Olivia if I could go?"

"No. I just thought of it this minute. You know me—impulsive is my middle name."

"James and Olivia think your middle name is professional tourist."

"Ha! They would. We'd have fun, though, wouldn't we?"

"But they said I have to help in the clinic every Sunday this month. They're understaffed because of the holiday."

"Well, never mind. I'm coming through Banda Aceh again on my way back to the States next Tuesday. We'll see each other then."

"I hate that you're going back to Boston without me. I thought you were on my side."

Matt laughed. "Don't hate me. I said I'd take you back with me. It was your folks who put their feet down. Personally, I think you've done your time here."

"I could finish the year at my old school," Emily began. She knew she wasn't persuading anyone now, but the plan was so perfect it needed to be aired just for its beauty. "I could live with you and help you with housework in exchange for room and board. I'd only be away from James and Olivia for four months."

"Yeah, yeah, yeah . . ."

"Just a little reprieve—that's all I'm asking," Emily said. "Just to have friends again, and to have a normal life."

"Sorry, Squirt, but my hands are tied. I've got to go. Hey, I left you a present on the kitchen counter."

Emily looked over her shoulder at a plastic jar of American peanut butter. The blue, red, and green label flooded her with the warmth of familiarity.

"Oh, Matt!" she said. "Thank you *so* much! And it's creamy!"

"You're welcome. Hang in there. I'll see you in a few days."

After Emily hung up, she made the most delicious dinner she had eaten in a long time: two thick peanut butter and honey sandwiches and a tall glass of milk.

A mosquito had made a meal of Emily as she slept. Late that morning, looking in the bathroom mirror at the red welts on her face, she began to cry quietly. As she cried, she couldn't help but notice how pitiful her reflection looked, sniveling alone in the bathroom in just a camisole. Finally she put on a tunic and leggings, splashed water on her face, dried herself, and joined her parents at the breakfast table.

"'Morning," Olivia said, cutting an orange.

Emily said nothing.

"Have you seen the cell phone, Emily?" James said. "I got a page from the clinic twenty minutes ago, but I can't find the phone."

"It's probably near my so-called bed somewhere. Matt called last night."

"What about?" Olivia said, laying the orange pieces on a plate. As she handed it to Emily, she noticed the welts.

"Oh, what's wrong with your face?" she asked, and then she answered the question herself. "Another monster mosquito in the house. I guess I should get some more mosquito coils."

"No, don't. They're a fire hazard," James called back. He was squatting, rummaging through Emily's clothes on the floor.

"The Tiger Balm is in the medicine cabinet, honey. That'll help," Olivia said to Emily, dumping some plates in the sink. Emily didn't move.

Olivia said, "Can you just grab a piece of toast and those orange slices? We're running late."

"I can't find the damn phone," James said.

"The page must be about Rabina," Olivia said, gathering her white coat and bag. "Let's just go. It would take less time than finding the phone. Come *on*, Emily, we're late!"

"Why can't you put the phone back in the kitchen?" James said to Emily.

Emily grabbed the scarf from the floor near her bed. She slid into her unbuckled sandals and took a piece of toast from the table.

They usually rode the van—a *bemo*—but a *becak* came right past the door as they stepped out, so Olivia flagged it down. This one had a lime green carriage and a black awning. The driver—a wiry, dusty, barefoot man— pulled it by peddling on a huge tricycle. It was designed to hold two people, but in a pinch, and for a couple hundred rupiahs more, an enterprising, energetic driver would allow James to hold his daughter on his lap.

Emily tied her scarf into a headdress as quickly as she

could. This time of the morning, there were plenty of people in the street who took notice of her, whizzing by, tall and fair and ungainly in her father's lap. Girls and their mothers peered out at her, dark-eyed and smiling from behind a curtain of thick Muslim veils. Thank God she was moving, Emily thought. If the *becak* driver were to stop for any reason, she knew that the children would gather around her asking questions about who she was, where she came from, where she was going, and could they touch her blond hair?

They rounded the corner past a white mosque and then pulled up in front of the hospital.

The night nurse burst out of the clinic. She was breathing hard and speaking quickly in Bahasa Indonesia. James and Olivia listened and then exploded into action. Emily stayed on the sidewalk outside the clinic to buckle her sandals.

Inside, she saw right away that Rabina's bed was surrounded by people, including James, Olivia, and the girl's mother and father, still dressed in their best clothes. She saw the nurse try to lead the parents away by their elbows, then give up. She heard her mother's voice, strained, in English to James, "She's in septic shock."

Amid the commotion, just next to the girl's cot, sat an old man on a woven rattan mat. He appeared to be in a trance, rocking gently forward and back. Next to him on the mat, an incense burner let off a thin stream of smoke that blew apart every time a nurse or Emily's parents reached past it.

"Emily!" Olivia barked. "There are beds full of other children. Can't you help?"

Emily heard a fragment of a sentence from the night nurse, ". . . tried to page you . . ."

And then her father's voice, in Bahasa Indonesia, "We cannot move her yet . . ."

Emily edged over to Yaso's bed. He was captivated by the commotion. He didn't seem to need anything.

She glanced at the broom standing in the corner. Sometimes Emily tidied up, but there was no mess this morning. She could check on the children in the other beds . . .

She heard the nurse's voice, ". . . sixty over thirty!"

Someone said, "Dear God."

Emily tilted her head and could barely see Rabina's face, covered with a plastic oxygen mask. Her black hair was in clumps on the pillow.

Then the girl was in cardiac arrest.

Between busy adults, Emily could see the girl's sheet pulled well away to reveal her bony chest. The oxygen mask flew to the floor. James's face and body were hidden from Emily's view behind the nurse, but Emily saw his big hands clasped together, palms down, beginning to press rhythmically on her chest. The depressions he made were so deep it looked as though he might crush her chest, snapping those fragile ribs. After every fifth depression, Olivia put her mouth over the little girl's mouth and blew.

It went on forever. The small woman in the *sarung* stood with her head buried in her husband's chest. The husband stood watching, still as a statue, as if invisible hands held him tight, forcing him to look. The old man rocked gently on his mat.

Emily didn't know what to do, so she sat in a chair by the wall and hugged her knees to her chest.

An hour later James and Olivia gave up. They recorded the time, and James turned to talk to the parents. Olivia carefully wrapped the girl in a white sheet so that she looked almost like a swaddled baby. She stood looking down at Rabina, with her hand resting lightly on the girl's shoulder. She reached out with one hand and gently tucked a wayward strand of Rabina's hair behind her ear.

The old man came out of his trance, put out the incense, and rolled up his mat. He bowed deeply to Rabina's parents and then offered his right hand, Western style, to James. James shook it and bowed his head slightly. Then the old man left.

All at once Emily noticed that there were children crying in the beds around her. She put her legs down and sat up straight, dazed.

Rabina's mother opened her little girl's swaddling sheet and folded it around her again so that her face was covered. Rabina's father lifted his daughter, light as a feather, as if he were carrying a toddler, and they left. Olivia followed behind them.

The day nurse arrived and began morning rounds.

James walked over to Emily.

"I'm so sorry the other children saw that," he said in a low voice, patting Emily's back.

"What could I have done?" Emily asked defensively.

"It's not your fault—we didn't have time to move her to a separate room." He stood thinking, pushing up his glasses with his middle finger. "I suppose you could have gotten the screen we use for privacy when a patient is bathing . . ."

"Nobody asked me to get the screen!" Emily said, panicked. "I was trying to stay out of the way!"

"I know. It's just an afterthought; there's no reason we can't learn from this."

"It seemed bad enough to me that the old *dukun* was in the way. I didn't want to make matters worse!"

"The *dukun* was not in the way, Em," James said.

"He was in the way! If that had been me, you would have yelled at me to get out of the way!" She was flushed red in the face. She couldn't stop herself. "How could you let him sit uselessly in the way? No, he was even worse than useless! He's the reason she was so sick!"

James crossed his arms and spoke with thin lips.

"Emily, many families can't afford to travel to hospitals, so they trust the folk remedies. They have to. The medicine of a good *dukun* is often very appropriate."

"How can you say that? You're a real doctor! How can you say that, now that Rabina is . . ."

She couldn't bring herself to say it. Her throat burned. She bit her lip.

"Rabina's parents needed him there," James said with finality. "They needed us, but they also needed him. Someday I hope you'll understand."

Emily couldn't speak. She couldn't think.

"We have work to do," James said. And then softly, "Please, Em . . . can you just get to work?"

Emily swallowed hard.

"I'm sorry about the phone," she croaked.

"What?"

She cleared her throat. "The phone. I'm sorry that I misplaced it."

She looked over at Rabina's empty cot. All that was left was the debris from trying to save her life. Who knows what James and Olivia could have done with those extra twenty minutes after the clinic paged them? Was it actually Emily's fault that Rabina was dead? Her eyes filled with hot tears. Without knowing where she was going, she turned and stumbled out the door.

She thought she heard her mother call to her.

Around the corner and a block down, she ran past the mosque. High up in the minaret, singing in Arabic, a *muezzin* chanted the noon call to prayer. He had a rich, plaintive voice that seemed to fall on her like a blanket. Emily covered her ears.

A *bemo* was parked just past the mosque. A hand-written sign in the window of the van read KRUENG RAYA and then in parentheses, in English, HARBOR.

5

It was the Islamic month of Ramadan. There were hundreds of people waiting to get on the ferry. It was a time when families traveled to see their relatives or visit the graves of their ancestors, or just went on holiday. Emily knew there might be standing room only on the boat, and most likely she and the other passengers would be packed together, skin to skin.

It was hardly a "boat," this ferry. Before she boarded, Emily saw it approach from the horizon. It was leaning to one side, like a bloated, sick whale slowly beaching itself at the dock. When it pulled in close, Emily could see that the weathered metal exterior had been patched here and there with solder, and one large hole had been filled with cement. She could barely make out the name,

Tandemand, handwritten in blistered paint on the hull. It was dirty inside. She swallowed hard.

A family pushed its way in alongside her. The father took one of the last spaces on the crowded stairs; the mother, surrounded by bags, leaned in a doorway with a baby girl on her hip. Two boys sat near her on the floor of the lower deck, with their bony knees up and the soles of their sandals down, whispering lively stories in each other's ears. It was noisy and hot, with the moist smell of many people in one place.

Emily fought a sudden, pressing urge to leave. She had been on ferries like this one at least a dozen times in the year and a half she had lived in Indonesia. One of those trips was this exact crossing—from Bandah Aceh on the northern tip of Sumatra to the small island of Weh. But she had always been with her parents before. This time she felt like she was suffocating, surrounded by all these people.

Well, she tried to reason calmly, she was on board now. She had paid her fare; there was no sense in turning back. She knew that Matt would take care of her, and she knew that she'd find him. Weh was a small island, and Sabang was a small town. Anyway, she knew which *losmen* he was staying in and, after all, she could easily locate him just by asking around. Indonesians notice all strangers, and word of their arrival spreads quickly. She smiled wryly. Matt—loud, American Matt—would definitely be a stranger to them.

Emily wished that she blended better with the crowd. She was tall, even for an American girl. It helped if she hunched, half-bowing at the waist as she passed adults; it was a sign of respect that sometimes prevented stares and whispers. So Emily used this gesture to find a space for herself on the upper deck, in the back with a lot of women and children, and she tried very hard to be small while they waited for the boat to set sail. After a few minutes she sat down with her knees up and rested her forehead on her folded arms.

Three hours later, they still had not set sail. Beepers went off, indicating an afternoon prayer time. Passengers washed their faces and hands, and even their feet, with bottled water. Some of the men unrolled mats or small woven rugs and aligned them in rows in the same direction. As they began their prayers, Emily turned her head away. She stretched to keep her legs from cramping, and then she mulled over her predicament.

She wasn't really a runaway. After all, she was just going on a tourist jaunt with Matt. Her parents might even find her absence a relief. That is, she thought sulkily, if they noticed her absence at all.

No, of course they'd notice. She wasn't there helping them, as she had promised. Still, they would probably assume she had gone home angry again, and they might not check on her until they finished their shift at the clinic. But that's good, Emily decided; she would call the house from the island. If it was early enough by the time she found Matt, she could call them at the hospital before they left for home. She would explain that Matt had invited her to Weh. Maybe Matt would be willing to soothe them, she brainstormed. Yes, she decided, he'd do that for her.

Having resolved that she was definitely not a runaway, the wait didn't bother Emily much. She was used to waiting in Indonesia. Things happened at a different pace here—*jam karet*, "rubber time"—a slow, tropical pace. Buses didn't show up on time, shops didn't open when their signs said they would, workers wandered to their posts when they were good and ready. There was no sense in Emily being impatient; it wouldn't get her anywhere any faster. Instead she stood up and looked across the channel at Weh. From the upper deck you could see the little island during the whole trip. Knowing Matt was there that very minute was almost like looking right at him. She could practically touch the island, it seemed so close. She'd be there soon.

She heard a voice behind her.

"Well, we could spot you across the deck, couldn't we?"

Emily turned around to face a man and woman. The man was cheerful and grinning; the woman quiet, but open. He had a dark salt-and-pepper beard and a cap that said BBC; she was wearing shorts and hiking boots. They were plump and tanned and very Western.

"It took us a while to make our way over here—it's so damned crowded on this ferry, though I suppose that's what we get for traveling during Ramadan. . . ." He stopped talking.

"Oh, sorry," he said. "Don't you speak English?"

"Yes, I'm American." Emily nodded.

He laughed. "You just surprised me there—you're so . . . lanky and fair, I couldn't imagine you'd be Indonesian, yet you didn't say anything for a moment."

Emily looked at the woman, who offered, "It wasn't a very long moment, Richard." She smiled at Emily and held out her hand. "I'm Catherine Richardson, and this my husband, Richard. He's rather outgoing—could you tell?"

Emily shook Catherine's hand, and then Richard's. Emily thought, even his name is talkative: Richard Richardson. Does he know Indonesians find his beard repugnant? Does Catherine know that only *becak* drivers and field workers wear shorts? Yet they seem so sure of themselves . . .

Catherine put her arm around Richard's waist and pulled him close. Emily watched nervously. It had been a long time since she had seen a couple embrace affectionately—other than her parents in their own home. In Indonesia it was common for women to hold hands with other women, or even for men to link arms with other men; such casual intimacy came naturally to them and was genuine and warm. But couples should never touch or hold hands in public. Emily looked around her, hoping that the other passengers weren't watching.

Richard was studying her.

"So I'll ask you the question these locals can't stop asking us—even though we're on the same blasted ferry going to the same blasted place, aren't we—where are you going?"

"Oh!" Emily smiled. "That's just a kind of greeting, like 'How are you?'"

"Fancy that," Catherine said.

"But to answer your question, I'm going to Weh to . . . to meet my uncle. And you?"

"We're off for a little holiday from our holiday," said Richard. "We hear Weh is lovely—like a Caribbean port if you go to Sabang—so that's where we're headed. We were in Medan yesterday, waiting for a flight out to Malaysia . . ."

Catherine interrupted, "But the bedbugs chased us out."

Richard said, "We were misinformed about the hotel, to say the least. . . ." He scratched some small red bumps on the inside of his elbow.

"I think we got the name wrong, Richard."

But he went on, "And the fact that there isn't a tree in that whole forsaken town, and it's loud and dusty, and the carbon-monoxide fumes . . ."

"Well, I wanted to get out of the city and go to the orangutan reserve, but Richard has had enough of trekking in rain forests for a while."

Emily said, "The reserve in Bukit Lawang? That's too bad; it's beautiful there."

The British couple smiled. Richard said, "You do know your way around! Do you and your parents live here?"

"Well, yes, here and there, for most of my life. My parents work for World Physicians for Children. We're really from Boston."

"Ah, the WPC," Richard said with recognition. "Do-gooders."

"Richard!" Catherine said.

He looked at Emily, "Well, they are, aren't they, er — what *is* your name?"

"Sorry. It's Emily. Emily Slake."

"And you get to live here," Catherine said, looking around her. "What a life experience. I think it's wonderful."

Richard said with some conspiracy, "But, Emily, when was the last time you had a good, fatty, American hamburger and chips, hey?"

The boat lurched forward out of the dock. The buzz among the passengers got louder over the sound of the straining engines. People began to settle themselves, as if now they knew they'd stay.

"Finally!" Richard raised his arms to the heavens. "Catherine said we ought to get off this old bucket, that it isn't seaworthy, but I knew it would sail . . . in its own sweet time."

The water was calm, and there was a light, humid breeze that evening. The ferry moved steadily, but not quickly, through the water. The sun was getting lower; it had been such a long wait on the dock. Emily wondered if she'd arrive too late to call Olivia and James at work. Would it be hard to find Matt once she arrived? She decided it would be safest to wait for him at his *losmen* until he turned in for the night.

Richard and Catherine paid two Indonesian passengers out of pocket to give up their seats on the deck near Emily. Emily stood, or sat on the floor with the other children. Catherine chatted with her. Richard alternately interjected and read his guidebook.

"That's pretty," Catherine said, pointing to Emily's headdress. Emily cringed. It wasn't polite to point with

31

your index finger in Indonesia; you were supposed to use your right thumb. She touched her *kerudung* nervously, in the front near her brow, as if to check that it was still there.

"The local women who work with my parents showed me how to wrap it. It's a traditional fabric," Emily said. Then she added almost to herself, "It's kind of hot right now, though."

"What do you do for schooling?" Catherine asked her. "Not that you aren't getting an education just by being here."

"We're homeschooling," Emily answered. "We get the books from my school, and I follow along from here."

"So your parents teach you?"

"Mmm . . . no. Well, yes. When they have time, I guess."

Richard looked up from a map. "What year would you be in now? Tenth? Eleventh?"

Emily felt her face get warm. "No, I'm just tall. I'm in ninth grade."

"Oh my! A wee babe. Well then, Richard and I must take care of you on this ride, mustn't we?"

Richard laughed. "Or the other way round, hmm? I'll bet *she* speaks the local dialect fluently. Better than our silly phrase books!"

They were quiet. The boat seemed to list to one side. The change was very slow at first, hardly noticeable. But after a few minutes, they were distinctly on the low end. Catherine squirmed in her seat.

"This is a lot, isn't it, this tilt? Do you think it's O.K.?"

A crewman walked briskly past with his brow furrowed. Emily heard a passenger ask him what was happening.

"No problem," he mumbled in Bahasa Indonesia, not looking up, not slowing his pace. "No problem," he said a little louder over his shoulder, as if it were an announcement.

Emily translated for Catherine.

"That man in the uniform says everything is fine."

She remembered the way the boat had looked as it approached the dock. And now it was certainly overloaded, but by how much? Had they distributed the cargo unevenly at the dock? She didn't wonder aloud. Catherine was chewing the cuticle around her thumbnail.

The tilt became more pronounced. Emily's heart raced. The same crewman returned, his forehead dappled with sweat droplets. He raised his voice. First in Bahasa Indonesia and then in broken English he said, "Moving to other side of boat. Be quick! Moving to other side of boat!"

The passengers moved, but they were unorchestrated and inefficient. They rushed this way and that, collecting their belongings, bumping into each other, and calling out to family members who were separated from them in the clamor.

Richard yelled, "The first-class lounge on the high side is practically empty—let's duck in there!" He grabbed Catherine's hand and dragged her through the crowd with his left arm stretched out in front of him as if he were a defensive linebacker. But like the Red Sea parted by Moses, a crowd of people poured in after the British couple, and Emily couldn't follow. She saw Catherine look back for her, and then she was gone.

The best Emily could do was to pick her way to the high side of the deck. She was trying to stay calm, but she was breathing fast, and she felt nauseated. The boat was at an unnatural angle now—the high side was very much out of the water—and she had to hold on to the railing to steady herself. Bags slipped down the deck. A boy next to her who was thin as a reed was hanging on to the same railing with his legs dangling freely at one moment, and his feet scrambling up the incline at the next. Oh my God, she thought, he's barely holding on. Then, silently and with great focus, the captain appeared, staggering against the tilt, making his way to a large locker mounted on the outer wall of the cabin. He opened it, reached inside, and began handing out life vests, which were packed inside the locker two deep and three across. Emily closed her eyes. This can't be happening, she said to herself. A little voice in the back of her head said with excruciating calmness, *What a shame, what a waste, if this boat sinks.*

She opened her eyes again, and now the captain was throwing vests willy-nilly to the crowd. One landed in her face, and she grabbed it with her free hand. She didn't hesitate. She didn't really even think. She hooked her arm through the railing to free up both hands and pushed the vest over the boy's head. He was screaming something at her, trying to shove her away but also hold the railing. She struggled to clip the front, then tried to reach the strap that would pull up through his legs. He kicked her hard in the face—so hard for such a waif!—and her arm unhooked from the railing. She lost her balance, stumbling down the hill of the deck straight into passengers, falling through them, knocking many down.

"*Ma'af!*" she yelled, as she barreled past, "Sorry!"

She tumbled until she arrived at the locker that held the life vests, but she was now on her stomach. She couldn't see inside it. She fought to stand. Someone fell on her, and she was down again. It was a man with wide eyes, large and round with fear. She cried out as she rolled from under him. She scrambled to her feet and peered into the locker. It was deep, dark, and seemed to be empty. And she had given her vest away! She bent at the waist, stretching her arms into the darkness, trying to feel for a vest on the floor of the locker. She looked over her shoulder as she groped, hoping to see a seat cushion, checking the walls for a life ring, for anything. There was a flash of yellow. She was pushed inside the locker — by a person falling against her or by the force of the boat tipping, she couldn't tell — and the locker door swung closed behind her.

Emily instantly reached her arms around and in front of her, but she could feel that the locker door was shut and there was no latch inside. In all the chaos no one on the outside could or would open it for her.

In a moment seawater had filled the locker through the seams and vent holes. It happened so quickly that she had time only to catch one shallow breath—half air, half water—before she was submerged. So it was true. The ferry was really sinking, and her parents were out there, less than eighteen miles away on the island of Sumatra, and they might never know what happened to her.

She began to kick the locker door. There was just enough room to brace her back, raise her knee, and push hard against the door with her foot, over and over. It felt like her leg was moving through the water in slow motion. An angry voice yelled, *Kick harder, Emily! Kick the door off its hinges! Get out of here!* at the very same time that a calm voice said, *It won't open. This is what it's like to die, but it will be O.K. It will be quick.* The voices were both hers.

How long could she hold her breath? she wondered. Isn't four minutes the longest a human brain can go without oxygen? A flash went through her mind of a film of tanned children with coarse black hair—pearl divers in Polynesia—holding their breath for nearly three minutes while they rummaged through the reef to earn money for their families. She had seen it in a documentary. These children, who had no time or money to go to school, broke their eardrums and risked their lives for pearls and still had almost nothing to show for it. *You see there,* said the gentle voice in her head, *you had time to dwell on those Polynesian children before you died.*

Her body wanted air so badly, just a little bit of air. Her mind knew better, but her mouth opened anyway. Water poured in and clutched at her throat until she coughed out the last of her used, stale air—air she wanted to keep!—and swallowed another mouthful of salt water. She kicked some more, this time violent, angry kicks. *Damn . . . those . . . Polynesian . . . children . . . damn . . . them . . . all!* screamed the angry voice with each kick.

The next thing she was aware of was being near the surface, choking, searching for air, and then vomiting. How could she be sick in the water without holding on to anything? It was a joke; she was heaving and drowning at the same time. Her wet clothes were so heavy they clawed her down under the water like huge hands, pulling her while she thrashed against them just to keep her head up, to breathe what felt mostly like foam and water while she starved for air.

She tipped her head back and pushed it up to the surface as hard as she could, pursing her lips above the swell and gulping real air before allowing herself to sink under again. She held her breath while she pulled her long tunic over her head and abandoned it. Then, free of that dead weight, she swam up for what seemed like an eternity, with her chest so achingly empty it felt as if it had collapsed, seeing only white bubbles in front of her face until she broke the surface. She spluttered and coughed, gasping for air.

But she was saved. She was saved.

She kicked off her left sandal. The other sandal was gone already, perhaps caught on the locker, and her right foot was cut and bleeding, she couldn't tell how much. She was wearing just her leggings now, and a scant, sleeveless undershirt. The *kerudung* had been ripped off her head somewhere between the locker and the surface. At last, she could freely tread water. Greedy for more than just air, now that she had plenty of that, she wished more than anything that she had a life vest. She looked around her.

It was dusk. There was a glow of orange and red on the horizon, with garishly pink, wispy clouds above the glow. People were moving all around her, floating and trying to keep afloat. There were splashes and yelling, and a queer sound of fizzing as trillions of tiny bubbles escaped from the sinking ferry. There were bodies, face-down in the water, bobbing in the waves. And there was the sun on the horizon, setting as lovely as could be, inching the Andaman Sea toward darkness, as if there were nothing out of the ordinary on this January evening.

The ship was upside down now, with the bottom sticking out of the water, rolling back and forth at a very low frequency. People were trying to climb on the bottom, to pull themselves out of the water.

Why were they even near it? Emily wondered. Surely they could see it was going to sink! The ones who managed to pull themselves onto the ferry bottom were standing, helping to pull up their friends and family and pushing strangers away. Emily looked around in desperation. If only the rescue boats were here, if only someone could make them all calm, save them before they hurt themselves, make them do the right thing.

But what was the right thing? Emily didn't know.

She was crying now, heaving, hot sobs that made her choke on her own mucus.

"Olivia! James!" she called, just to hear their names. Then she went under. She had been crying too hard, so hard that she couldn't catch her breath, and her airless body had sunk like a rock.

No! the angry voice in her head spoke up. *No! I won't drown! I won't let you drown!* She came up to the surface, took a huge breath, coughed up a wad of the thick crying-mucus, and spat it out.

"Idiot!" she hissed at herself. No crying, she thought. She had come this far and all she had to do was *hold on* until the rescue boats arrived.

The ferry made an ominous groaning sound along with the bubbly noises. She could feel the vibration through her body. Her instinct was to swim away from it, as fast as she could and without looking back. It was going down. She didn't want to be sucked under with it. She didn't want to know if the people were still on it. All those people who were standing on it . . . no, it was better not to know.

Then she remembered her British couple.

"Catherine! Richard!" she called. If only she could be with them. They could help her. Hadn't they said they would take care of her?

Oh God, but what if they hadn't made it? Had they gone inside that first-class lounge? How could they find their way out? What if the boat flipped all the way over while they were still inside? She couldn't remember whether the boat had been upside down when she was kicking the locker door. Perhaps it was, and the first-class lounge was filled with water too . . .

"Richard! Catherine!" she yelled, desperately now. She knew she could hang on if she had company. If only she had company.

Company! Ha, her angry voice said. *Look around you, there's company everywhere!*

The people in the water had started chanting now.

La ilaha illa Muhammad Rasul Allah.

There was wailing and moaning and crying, but also the rhythmic prayer chant of dozens of people.

La ilaha illa Muhammad Rasul Allah.

It was so moving and at the same time so hopeless. She wished they would stop. Allah would want them to do something besides pray, wouldn't he? Something to save themselves, and to help the people around them? No, maybe he does want prayer. Maybe he's a selfish god. Or maybe they thought praying was all they had. She didn't know.

Suddenly, she heard her name. She caught her breath. It was Richard!

"I'm here! I'm here!" she screamed. "Richard!"

"Thank God, she made it," she thought she heard — was it Catherine's voice?

Emily yelled, "It's getting too dark. I can't find you! Where are you?"

They called to Emily, both of them — Catherine *was* there! — and she swam for their voices. When she reached them, Catherine was crying. Neither Richard nor Catherine was wearing a life vest.

"Oh God, Emily. Oh God. You're O.K.," Catherine said.

They couldn't hug; it would drag them down. So Emily and Catherine reached out a hand to each other and squeezed tightly, briefly.

"Don't worry, Emily," Catherine said, but her voice was quavering. "We've all got off the boat, we haven't sunk with the boat, and we found each other. . . ." Her voice trailed off.

Richard said, "Look, we've got to stay positive. We're going to make it." He turned to Emily, or rather to Emily's shadow. It was the kind of evening light where you can see things better out of the corner of your eye, where only movement lends shape to an object.

"You Americans are great. I just love you guys. Look at what a strong swimmer you are, and you're just a kid. It's that pioneer pluck . . . it's in your blood." He stopped.

Emily didn't respond. The sounds of the other passengers were penetrating her, pushing themselves to the front of her brain, shouting over her body's adrenaline.

La ilaha illa Muhammad Rasul Allah.

"I saw this video once," he went on quickly, "this American videotape. It was all about racecar crashes. The whole thing! One crash after another, with fire and smoke, and cars flipping around in midair . . . just insane! And there was this voice-over—an excitable chap with this high-pitched voice; he was so bloody loud!—and every time there was a crash he would scream, '*And he walked away!*' about the driver, because somehow, miraculously, each time they had escaped being killed."

Emily grunted. They were in the middle of the ocean, treading water, next to a sunken ferry and hundreds of helpless, dying passengers. What was he telling her?

"That's—that's what I'm going to say to you both the moment we get out of this mess, I promise you," he said earnestly. '*And she walked away . . .* '"

Catherine had been silent for too long.

"Luv?" Richard said to his wife in the darkness.

"I'm cold," she answered.

"Oh, you can't be!" he said with a chipper voice. "This water has to be thirty degrees centigrade . . ."

"No, I'm shaking. I'm cold," she insisted. Her voice was trembling, and Emily wondered if Catherine was in shock.

"Look! There's a life raft there!" Richard shouted to Catherine and Emily.

It must have been a raft; it couldn't have been anything else, because there were shadows of many people, in a clump, thrashing above the water, swaying back and forth in the swells.

Richard led the way toward the raft. They swam through a debris field of shoes, scarves, and paper cups: useless debris. Everything that could be used as a flotation aid had been taken.

As they approached the life raft, Emily stayed back behind Catherine, who was following Richard. Emily heard men shouting at each other in Bahasa Indonesia, "Get off! Get off! Let go!" Others were screaming, "Move over! Let me on!" Many of them were shoving hard, pushing and pulling, or hanging off the sides, and some who had already staked a claim were kicking the heads and hands of the hangers-on. The tiny raft looked as if it would be torn apart. It wasn't that big to begin with. There were at least twenty people fighting over it, and it was upside down.

Richard was frantic. Catherine felt nauseated. She had lost both of her contact lenses, she was no longer treading water well, and now she was shaking uncontrollably. Richard threw himself into the fray.

"Either get on or get off!" Emily heard him yell in English. "You're going to sink this damn thing!" But no one listened to him.

"Stop hanging on the edge! You're going to pull it over!"

He pushed a man away from the edge. The man shoved him back and shrieked at him, clawing at his face. Richard pushed him again, and grabbed Catherine by the arm.

Emily watched as he pushed her from below, up and onto the raft, fighting off other men at the same time. Catherine was bent at the waist, with her legs hanging in the water and her face in the depression of the raft, unable to lift herself, stuck halfway. A man in the raft started to heave her overboard, like an unwanted sack.

"Stop it! Have you gone mad?" Richard yelled. "Listen, she's a lady! She's got to—she should be in the raft!"

"Let her on," a man yelled in Bahasa Indonesia.

The first man said in English, "No more! No more!" and began pushing Catherine again. Richard screamed. It wasn't words; instead, it was almost like a tribal war cry, a primitive sound from deep in his chest. He lifted himself up on the side of the raft using one arm and began punching the man who was pushing Catherine. He dragged him down by the hair and pounded on him with wild, flailing punches. Emily saw the silhouette of his arm, powerful and fisted, like that of a gorilla beating the ground to stake its territory. The fist rose and fell an agonizing number of times, but Emily couldn't tell which blows hit their mark. In the end Richard pulled the man right off the raft.

Emily watched in horror. One of them was going to drown. She didn't want it to be Richard, but she couldn't hope for it to be the other man, either. She turned away; she had to. She swam away from the raft, her heart beating so hard that it felt like it was pounding against the skin of her chest. When she was far enough away that the people and the raft would be just a blur of shadows, she turned around. For a while, mercifully, she saw nothing in the darkness.

Then she saw the shadow of an arm waving to her from the water next to the raft. It was Richard's arm. He had won a place for Catherine.

"Emily! Emily!" Richard was yelling to her from the distance. "Come on the raft!"

"How?" she screamed back. How, she thought, without causing a fight, a deadly fight, and risking not only Richard's life, but hers and Catherine's as well if Richard lost? How, without having to watch someone die?

She swam closer to the raft, but stayed a safe distance from the swarms of people who were around it, still clamoring for a space. Their desperation scared her. With no earth beneath their feet, no dry clothes, no loved ones, they had lost control of themselves. A frantic voice inside her head said, *Don't lose Richard and Catherine. How can you save yourself if you don't get on that raft?* But she was so confused. Even Richard had gone a little crazy, hadn't he?

"I'll stay nearby!" she yelled.

"What?" he screamed over the shouts and splashes. "Emily!"

"I'm here! Don't worry!"

Best to keep an eye on them, to stay near enough that she could find them, but not so near that she would threaten the keepers of the raft.

But she was getting tired. She was still wearing the thin undershirt and her leggings, and they felt heavy. She tried to remember the lifesaving unit she'd had in school back in the States. There were ways of treading water that used less energy. What were they? She had never been very good at floating on her back. Maybe because her legs were so long, or because she didn't have enough body fat. It always felt like she was sinking, unless she inflated her lungs with so much air that they buoyed her torso, in which case she exhausted herself by holding her breath. This was how she had managed to fake her way through the back float during the class, but it was useless to her now.

She was good at sculling her arms to tread water. She knew to keep it rhythmic and slow, making the shape of a flattened figure eight with her hands, and to use a scissors kick with her legs. And she had a good breaststroke, which she knew was one of the least tiring strokes that still gives you forward motion. She could do the breaststroke all day if she had to. She could also kick on her back, sculling with her hands down by her hips. If necessary, she would do the sidestroke just to use a different set of muscles.

She wished she could take off her clothes. The air and water were both warm; she didn't really need clothes. Yet she couldn't be rescued naked, could she? Would an Indonesian rescuer be willing to pull her into a boat with all of her skin showing? But of course she would be saved, naked or not. This was an emergency; surely there was some leeway in the local customs if it was a matter of life and death.

In the lifesaving class, wasn't there some way you could use your clothes to your advantage? Something to do with pants . . . or jeans. Yes—if you tie knots in the legs and capture air in your jeans, they'll float. Enough to hold most of your body weight, if you do it right.

No one was near her. She took off her leggings. They were cotton and spandex. A tight weave, but thin material— not even close to denim. Would it work? She knotted the legs near the knees, and gathered the waist into one hand, like a balloon opening. Then she blew into them while treading water. They did hold the air, but it wasn't much, and she couldn't figure out how to knot the waist, so she just held it closed in her hand.

In this way the leggings did work as a small float. She still had to tread water, but the makeshift balloon took some of her weight and made the work easier. She felt as if she had accomplished something, and that was a good feeling. It was the first really calm thing that she had done to help herself, wasn't it?

She looked around her. It was nearly dark. The chanting had stopped for the moment. It came and went, and each time fewer voices joined in. Emily didn't want to think about what that meant. She spun her body in a slow circle, looking out toward where she thought the horizon would be, searching for rescue boats that still were not there.

9

It was completely dark. The stars were beginning to show, and there was the promise of a glow from a moon that had not yet risen. Emily couldn't see her watch, but she guessed that she had been in the water for more than two hours. The ferry probably sank sometime after five o'clock. In a couple of hours I should be getting to bed, she thought, then shook her head at how ridiculous that was. Or, how ridiculous *this* was, really, floating in the ocean, holding a blown-up pair of leggings, afraid of the people around her, yet more afraid of not being near them.

There had been hundreds of people on the ferry, but now the sounds of voices had diminished to practically nothing, and she didn't know why. Had everyone drowned? It was too horrible a thought. All those women and children. She closed her eyes to push away the image of the whispering boys, and of their mother with the baby on her hip.

Had the others begun swimming in the direction of shore? Where *was* the shore and how far away . . . how could they? After the sinking, many of the passengers that Emily could see in the water still had all their clothes on; she remembered how heavy her own tunic had been. How could they swim like that? Some would not be able to swim at all; Emily knew that unpredictable currents, dangerous tiger sharks, and personal modesty kept many Indonesians from learning how to swim.

But maybe she had simply drifted away from the majority of the survivors in her effort to keep her distance. No, she didn't think so. She hadn't actively swum anywhere. She had tried to stay in one place.

She couldn't see the shadows on the raft, but she frequently called out to Richard and Catherine, or they called anxiously to her, and she would memorize their bearing and try to stay near. Catherine had stopped begging Emily to come to the raft; Richard, in the water alongside his wife, had already had two more scuffles to keep Catherine's place secure, and there was no realistic way that Emily could get on board. The truce that Richard had with the other raft passengers was uneasy at best.

She felt the cool, smooth touch of a jellyfish gently brush against her in the current, causing a prickly burning across the front of her thighs and on the top of her left foot. If she had been at the beach, she would have doused the wound with vinegar. She would have gotten out of the water immediately and nursed her rash for days.

Instead she distracted herself from the ache by looking up at the stars. She leaned back and sculled with her free hand—the hand that was not holding the leggings-float—doing a gentle frog kick with her legs whenever they sank too low. Soon she discovered a new position, with her head tilted back and her body and legs hanging down at a forty-five-degree angle. If she kept her lungs full and breathed very shallowly, she could stay afloat without any sculling or kicking. It was almost effortless. With her ears submerged she could hear only the sound of her lungs, loud and functional and rhythmic, as if through a stethoscope.

As her eyes became accustomed to the night sky, more stars slowly appeared, until there was a blanket of them over her. In fact, in the clear air, away from any lights, with the night settling itself deeply in, there were millions of them. Of course, more than millions— uncountable, everyone knew. The more she looked, the more it seemed as if there were actually no areas of empty space around the stars; there were so many stars behind, next to, and in front of the others that they were contiguous. It was like a pointillist painting, covered so perfectly with dots of color that none of the canvas showed. But in this living painting of the night sky over Indonesia, the dots were all one color—the color of brilliant, distant suns.

Suns, all of them, like our own sun, she thought. Galaxies upon galaxies of suns of every imaginable type and age. Some surely with planets around them, planets capable of supporting life. Even if it were just amebic life forms—single cells—still it was life as valuable in the grand scheme of things as life on earth. It was life that struggled, that evolved, that tried to pass on a bit of itself to the next generation. If it was intelligent life, it probably loved, it knew family, it suffered sadness, disease, or even war?

If there was a god, these life forms on other planets were generated by him, just as likely as he generated life on earth. Or wouldn't you rather say that he generated the conditions — atmospheric gases, climate, water, soil — that would sustain life? That way you could believe in evolution *and* God. Emily's lips curled wryly. Could she be the first person to figure out a way that creationism and science can coexist? The Bible said that Adam was created in the image of God, and Eve from Adam's rib. Couldn't this just be poetic license on the part of the authors, who didn't really know any science? Couldn't you believe in evolution and God if you accepted that God orchestrated the big bang and everything that followed naturally from that?

Surely some adult philosopher or theologian had thought of this already. She was just a kid — what did she know? But if they hadn't — she smirked again — she'd have to make sure she survived this ordeal to write some kind of masterpiece blending Darwinism and creationism. Girl Genius, she imagined the headline, Has Revelation while Stranded in Ocean.

She looked at her wrist. Still too dark to see her watch. Well, maybe she had successfully passed all of four minutes solving the mystery of life. She wondered how much longer she would have to wait. It would be a grave injustice, wouldn't it, if after all this the rescue boats didn't find her?

She focused on the stars again, and one little point of light moved down in a streak. For a fraction of a second she thought it was a plane, but it was clearly a shooting star. Half a minute later, another. The longer she looked, the more she saw. A beautiful light show, hundreds of miles away. No, not really a light show. These were bits of rock or dust, burning into nothing as they traveled through the earth's atmosphere. They were lifeless meteors that cared nothing for her. They weren't shooting for her; they weren't shooting for any human beings. They had shot long before humans were on earth, and they would shoot long after humans were gone. Look at that sky, millions of miles deep. Nothing in that incredibly full sky cares about humans, or about the silly, stupid things we do. Humans are the only things that care about humans, and in the end we don't even do that very well.

She suddenly felt very small, and very exposed. She stopped breathing and straightened up, pulling her legs up against her chest. But she couldn't both hug herself and stay afloat.

"Ri-chard?" she called out, her voice cracking.

Before she could hear an answer, she was pulled under the water. She didn't have time to catch a breath. Someone, some*thing* was dragging her under from behind. She felt water churning in front of her face. She scraped at the water with her hands, losing her leggings-float. She didn't feel any pain, but she was sure it was a shark.

If it was a shark, she thought, it would drag her down, taking a hunk out of her body, or taking off a leg. Wounds that large, that mortal, sometimes didn't hurt; there wasn't time. Then she'd be spat out, left to bleed to death in a matter of seconds.

Emily thrashed spastically underwater, and as she did she felt cloth intertwining around her legs and arms. This was no shark; this was a person holding her down, now with arms tightly around Emily's neck. It was a person who was drowning and trying to pull up out of the water by hanging on to Emily. They would both drown! She had to get away.

Emily kicked backward in the water at the person and flung her arms this way and that until she shook loose. She tried to swim away but was pursued by clinging hands that grabbed her undershirt and her underpants. She managed to turn herself to face the person, lift her legs, and kick with such force that she kicked herself free. She must have kicked the person in the belly, because she heard a *woomf* of air and bubbling voice underwater. Emily headed frantically for the surface. Once there, she gasped for air and swam away, so she wouldn't be caught off guard again.

For a moment she thought with dread that she might have kicked so hard that she had injured the person, enough for him or her to drown. But in a few seconds she heard gurgling and bubbles and choking, and in the faint light of the rising moon she saw a woman claw her way to the surface—as if she were climbing a ladder—and splash around frantically, looking for Emily.

"Stop!" Emily said in Bahasa Indonesia. "Stay away!"

The woman flailed. She was wearing too many clothes, and she swam inefficiently. How could she have survived all these hours, doing this exhausting, jerky dog paddle, with such heavy clothes?

"I need you . . . to help me," the woman said. "Please, please come here. Don't go away!"

"I cannot hold you and swim at the same time!" Emily said. "But I want to help you. . . . I want to help you!"

The woman tried to swim to her.

"Take off your *sarung!*" Emily commanded.

"You swim so well," the woman said, choking again on the water. "I never learned to swim properly . . ."

"You must take off your *sarung* now—it is heavy! Then I will show you how to swim better." Emily swam in small circles around the woman to stay clear of her.

"I'm too tired!" the woman yelled, now desperately. To Emily's horror, she sank under the surface, and the more she dog-paddled, the deeper she seemed to sink.

Emily froze with fear. The woman was drowning before her eyes. She couldn't just watch; she couldn't let her drown! But Emily was paralyzed, holding her breath. She had kicked and pushed the woman—so hard!—when the woman was already exhausted from hours of dog-paddling in her clothes, and now she was going to die because of Emily.

Move! Do something! Do anything! she heard in the back of her mind. She obeyed, diving under and pulling up whatever she could find, which seemed to be mostly the woman's *sarung*. The voice said, *Fine, pull the damned thing off!* so Emily did, yanking the cloth up so violently that the woman's arms were lifted over her head and the *sarung* got stuck halfway. The woman struggled and let out enormous bubbles of air as she fought.

Oh my God, Emily thought, I'm killing her! This isn't working!

Emily came up for air, let out a cry of anguish, and dove under again. The woman twisted and turned underwater while she sank deeper, but she could not have had a drop of air left in her. This time Emily felt in the darkness of the water until she found what she prayed was the end of the *sarung*, floating above the woman's head, and screamed underwater as she pulled it. She could feel it pop over the woman's head, but the woman's arms were still inside, pointing straight up. Emily kept pulling on the cloth, swimming up until she broke the surface of the water. Gasping, panicked, and shaking as she swam, Emily dragged the *sarung* in a frantic sidestroke, knowing the woman would follow in an arc, arms first, behind the cloth. The woman's face broke the surface and, on her back, she choked and vomited water.

Emily was desperate to get the *sarung* off so she could help the woman stay above water. The woman's arms were still over her head, stuck in the tight sleeves, but she floated on her back, choking and gasping for breath, as long as Emily kept swimming ahead of her, dragging her by the *sarung*.

Emily stopped swimming, held on to the end of the cloth with both hands, swung her legs up, and pushed against the woman's shoulders with her feet, peeling the sleeves off her arms like sausage casings. Then she grabbed the woman before she had a chance to sink under, and swam with the woman's head, faceup, in the crook of her elbow. She swam this way in large circles until the woman stopped choking.

Emily talked to her in Bahasa Indonesia.

"You are fine!" she panted. "You are doing very well. Everything is just fine now."

The woman didn't respond, but her choking eased.

"Yes, rest." Emily couldn't remember the word for "relax."

"You must be tired. You swam so long in very heavy clothes! But everything is just fine now."

The woman moaned, a long vibrato moan. She was trembling uncontrollably. Emily had run out of things to say, so she sang a song instead. The first quiet song she could think of.

> *Blackbird singing in the dead of night*
> *Take these broken wings and learn to fly*
> *All your life*
> *You were only waiting for this moment to arise.*

> *Blackbird singing in the dead of night*
> *Take these sunken eyes and learn to see*

All your life
You were only waiting for this moment to be free.

The woman grunted, like a baby at its mother's breast. Emily did not have enough breath to sing anymore. The more she swam holding the woman, the more the woman got a chance to rest, but Emily's muscles were sore, and she had almost completely lost her strength. It was time to teach.

"You must swim now," Emily said with a little gasp. "I am tired and I cannot swim for us both."

"No . . . no . . . no . . ." the woman said weakly.

"But I will show you how to swim better . . ."

"No . . ."

". . . and you are much, much more light now. It will be fine. It will be good."

"No!" the woman yelled as Emily let go.

"It will be fine!" Emily repeated firmly, easing away from her. But the woman immediately began to panic, clawing her arms up the imaginary ladder, trying to climb out of the water, trying to pull herself back to Emily.

"Stop making your arms like that!" Emily said. The woman sank under.

Emily swam to her, grabbed her from behind, and resumed the lifesaving swim.

"Listen to me! You must not reach up with your arms like that! You must keep them under the water and push them to the sides, gently! Do you hear me?"

"No . . . I cannot. I'm too tired! You must hold me!"

"I cannot hold you! I am tired! Now, this very minute, I am so tired—I cannot hold you!"

"I cannot swim anymore. I cannot swim," the woman said to the sky.

"You must swim or you will not live!"

"Then I will not live," said the woman, suddenly sober.

"You *will* live, if you try! Now remember—remember to push your arms to the sides." Emily let her go again.

This time the woman let herself sink into the water. It was deliberate, and—after all of her terror—it was eerily calm. Emily could not believe what she was seeing.

"Stop!" she screeched in English. "Stop it!"

She grabbed the woman again, but this time the woman fought her and pulled away. She let herself sink. Emily yelled, "No!" and reached for the woman once more, yanking her face out of the water by the hair.

The woman wrenched away from her with what looked like hatred in her eyes.

"Do not bring me back up again," she said through her teeth.

Emily watched as the woman sank in the water one last time. She squeezed her eyes tightly shut and turned away. She was shaking. Then she swam, using the crawl stroke, as hard as she could, away into the ocean. As she did, the song she had sung wound its way through her brain, tormenting her.

Blackbird fly, Blackbird fly
Into the light of the dark black night.

Blackbird fly, Blackbird fly
Into the light of the dark black night.

Emily put voice to her breath underwater, *hoam,* as she swam. She chanted in this way, rhythmically with each stroke, to fill the emptiness and to announce her presence to the ocean. Why had the woman given up? What if she had family somewhere, waiting for her, hoping and praying that she was alive? How could the woman have let them down like that? How could she have refused to help herself? It was like rejecting the gift of life, when so many others on the ferry had not even been offered the chance.

Emily knew that she couldn't let her parents down. She couldn't let anyone down. She had to get through this. She owed it to everyone after stupidly running away. The only way they would know she had come this far would be if she lived to be rescued.

Other people in the world had survived worse. Other people lived with challenges every day—if they were sick, or if someone they loved had died, or if they were poor and hungry. Their lives were a struggle every moment, and all she had to do was struggle a little while longer—she had already survived the worst of it, hadn't she?—and she'd be back, protected by her parents, with a home and food and clothes. God, she had so much. She would do anything to get back. When she was home, she could forget all about this. But she had to make it first. She had to make it.

The crawl stroke left Emily out of breath, and her lungs hurt. She eased into a slow breaststroke, then stopped swimming when she heard her name behind her in the distance. It was Catherine, and her voice seemed very small and far away. Emily realized she no longer knew where the raft was.

"Catherine?" she called.

"Emily!" she heard again, and this time she followed the voice.

The moon was high now, and it cast a blue light on her large, watery world. Soon Emily could see something floating between her and the raft. It was the woman, dead and facedown. She couldn't bear to swim past the body, so she swam to the side for a while to detour around it. As she did, Catherine kept calling to her. The voice was like a beacon, drawing her to safety and comfort.

Something caught on her hand as she swam and she recoiled from the touch. It was cloth. She lifted it out of the water. It was her leggings! A little gift from the ocean, a thing of hope. A good thing to follow the bad. She gathered the waist in her hand and blew up the pants again.

In the dim light she could see that the scuffle on the raft had reached a nervous equilibrium. Still overloaded, the raft was almost completely submerged under the weight, and it swayed precariously. There were still people hanging on it in the water, but they weren't fighting. They were lined up tightly around it, stomachs to backs, or face to face, each with only one hand holding the rope on the side. Some other men, better swimmers, were treading water near the raft. She envied the people holding the side of the raft. She had not stopped swimming or treading water for hours and she was tired. But she was grateful to have her leggings-float back.

She swam closer to the raft, then in a wide circle around it until she could make out the familiar shapes of Catherine and Richard among the others.

"I'm here; I'm here!" she called out. Richard was in the water, holding the side of the raft as she approached.

"Hi," Emily said weakly.

"Hullo, dear," Richard said warmly, then to Catherine, "Look, luv, she's fine. She's a born survivor, I told you." He looked back at Emily, "The Unsinkable Emily Slake. She's tough, she is."

Emily's eyes brimmed with hot tears. She swallowed hard. "No, I'm not," she said quietly. "I'm so tired. People are dying all around us. . . ." She thought of the desperate woman, but she couldn't talk about it. She couldn't spare any more of her energy for that woman, not now.

"Why aren't the rescue boats here?" She cringed at how whiny her voice sounded.

"Here, take a turn holding the side, and I'll have a turn swimming," Richard said. "We can switch off for as long as it takes." He put out his hand, and she reached for it. Then he pulled her in and they changed places. Emily heard someone near her growl almost imperceptibly. She shivered.

Emily held the rope of the raft with her right hand and kept the leggings inflated in her left. In that way, without having to kick her legs at all, she stayed afloat with blissfully little effort. Her heart rate slowed, and her breathing became regular. If the world could stay just like this for just long enough, she thought, she would survive to be rescued.

"If this were America there would be a hundred helicopters zooming overhead," Emily said to Richard, softly, in case the people around her spoke English.

"Yeah, television crews!" Richard boomed. Emily and Catherine laughed, a bursting laugh, a release of nervousness, and hopelessness, and frustration. Then they were quiet.

The people around them spoke in low tones. But much of the time everyone was quiet. Emily had heard that in World War II the survivors in British air raid shelters were often silent while the bombs were blasting above them. You might expect them to scream or cry, but in fact people were often quiet, just waiting—even children— knowing there was absolutely nothing more they could do. This is how they all felt now, Emily thought, she and Catherine and Richard, and the other raft dwellers. Not numb from cold, because it was warm enough, but numb from waiting, and accepting whatever the sea had to offer.

"Gosh, I'm hungry," Catherine said quietly. "Can you hear my stomach?"

Emily lifted her left arm to peer at her watch. For the first time since she had been on the boat, she could see the time in the moonlight. It was ten-forty.

"We missed supper," Richard agreed.

"I missed lunch," Emily said.

"Oh no! How did that happen?" Catherine said.

A little wave of panic overtook Emily. The truth was that she hadn't had enough money to buy lunch *and* a ferry pass because she had run away. Should she lie or be honest? In a fraction of a second, the choice became clear to her.

"I'd better tell you both the truth," Emily said, "in case I don't . . . get home for some reason. . . ." Her throat became tight.

"Don't be silly, dear!" Catherine interrupted.

"You'll make it all right," Richard said. "We'll see to that."

If only they could make that promise, Emily thought.

"Now, what's so important for us to know?" Catherine asked softly.

"I didn't have lunch because I didn't have enough money with me. Well, I had enough to buy a drink, that's all." She took a breath. "I sort of ran away," Emily said quietly. Then she added quickly, "Only sort of, because my uncle did invite me to meet him on Weh, and I'm sure that my parents would trust me to make the trip on my own if my uncle were meeting me. But I didn't ask them before I left, and I didn't settle it with my uncle."

Emily decided not to mention that she was angry and confused when she got on the *bemo*, and that a seven-year-old girl may have died because of her—a seven-year-old Emily's parents had fought for weeks to save. Those things weren't necessary. Those things could safely go down with her if she drowned.

Catherine said, "Oh, I see. Oh my, your parents must be worried sick that you're not at home."

"Probably not right now," Emily said. "I'm allowed to go many places alone, and they're working late tonight. Anyway, now you know why I need you to know. You're the only people in the world who could tell my parents that I . . . that I was on this ferry. Their names are James and Olivia Slake."

"James and Olivia Slake," Catherine repeated softly.

"We'll be glad to have you introduce us personally," Richard said firmly.

Emily looked into the sky, at the moon, nearly full and so large she could see the craters and plains more clearly than she had ever seen them before. She thought, there are human footprints up there right now in the powdery gray dust, and a flag. Isn't that amazing? She remembered seeing a photograph that was taken from the moon by an astronaut: there had been a monotone, craggy horizon of dead craters in the foreground, looking out into black space at a sparkling blue and green planet. The earth from that vantage had pure white clouds swirling over it in beautiful patterns, looking fresh and wonderfully alive and at peace. The astronaut had written about the photo later, saying something like, "We had come hundreds of thousands of miles to see the moon, and it was the earth that was worth looking at."

"Look, there's an aeroplane!" Catherine interrupted Emily's thoughts.

It wasn't a rescue plane. It was a passenger jet at very high altitude—just a blinking, slow-moving speck of light.

"Isn't it strange?" Emily said. "That people could be up there, flying home or on business, eating salted peanuts and drinking Coke out of a plastic cup, or reading or something? I mean, up there, there are flight attendants bringing people pillows and chatting with each other in the back of a plane . . ."

Emily stopped. They must think I'm crazy, she thought.

Richard said, "And here we are floating around a half-sunken raft in the pitch-dark, in the middle of the ocean . . ."

"Yeah," Emily said. "That those two things could be happening at the very same time. . . ." She shook her head at the thought. At that precise moment there were kids back home in Boston, laughing in the school cafeteria, or walking the halls, or daydreaming in class. Oh, if only she could transport herself, just blink herself like a genie onto that airplane or into that class. They were out there—all those other lives—happening right this minute, without her, totally unaware of her, wet and hungry and so tired. Why did she have to be here? She suddenly wanted more than anything to be dry and in her bed.

"It's strange to think about, all right," Catherine agreed. "Completely mad that we're here, really."

12

Emily's right arm was getting stiff. Hanging on to the rope on the raft was restful, but at a price. She felt uncomfortably close to the people holding on around her, as if she were being examined and judged unworthy of her spot, as if she were a cheater. After all, it was Richard who had fought for this space, not her. And she and Catherine were the only women on or near the raft that she could see in the dim light of the moon. She felt exposed in just her underpants and thin camisole.

The man in front of her seemed to have a silent collusion with the man behind her because they frequently kicked her, separately and underwater, as if by accident. They sandwiched her whenever the currents briefly pushed them into her space—so close that she could feel the breath of the man behind her on her neck—and one sniffed loudly while the other cleared his throat in her ear. Her heart raced, but she kept her head up and pretended not to notice.

"Hey, Richard? It's your turn now," she said.

"You O.K.?"

"Yeah! Yeah. I just feel like swimming for a while. My arm is stiff."

They exchanged places, and she was free. She stretched her arms a few times in a wide breaststroke. She blew up her leggings a little more. The breeze was stronger now, and the swells were growing, like giant undulating moguls on a ski slope.

After a few hours of this a person could get seasick, she thought. The last time she had gone skiing — how old had she been then, eleven? — she could feel the moguls in her sleep all night, as if her inner ear had been trapped in the rhythm of the slopes. She guessed that would probably happen to her again after she was rescued tonight.

She turned to approach the raft again. It was swaying in the swells. It was already almost completely submerged, and the swaying dipped the passengers deep in the water in a rhythmic motion. The people on top were getting nervous with each dip; it was slippery, and the waves were causing them to lean on each other. To make matters worse, they shifted their bodies — trying to regain their balance, trying not to fall, or just because they were anxious — and their movements combined with the swells to make the raft sway even more. Emily heard Richard try to quiet the passengers. Then she heard Catherine.

"Richard! There's a lot of big . . . fish in the water. Richard . . . Oh God, Richard, they're really big."

"It's O.K., luv. Stay still. Listen, they're dolphins. I can see them."

Emily instinctively clenched her fists. She couldn't see anything in the water around her. What had Catherine seen? She had an urge to be closer to Richard. He was so sure of everything; she needed to be near him.

Catherine said, "Dolphins?"

"Yes . . ." Richard began, but whatever he said next was drowned out by a scream on the raft. It was a man, yelling in Bahasa Indonesia, "Sharks! There are sharks!"

There was a sudden thrashing and splashing in the water — were the sharks attacking or were the people just panicking? The water churned. She saw several people fall off the raft in succession as it tipped wildly. The ocean was a moving wall around her. She choked on water spraying into her mouth. It was almost as if she were underwater; it was so hard to find a breath of real air among the waves. She gripped her leggings-float so tightly that her fingernails pressed into the palm of her hand. She looked frantically for Richard. She tried to cry out to him but swallowed a mouthful of salt water instead. She heard a hiss of air escaping from the raft — had it popped? She heard screams for help.

A man appeared in front of her. His eyebrows were furrowed, and his lips were pursed with effort. He was racing for her, and she couldn't swim backward fast enough. No, he was reaching for her leggings! How did he know she had them? He must have been one of the men who was near her at the side of the raft.

The man struggled through the waves to grasp her arm — the arm holding the leggings. She had to get away. Did he mean to drown her for her pitiful float, for a pair of flimsy pants? While there were sharks swirling in the water around them, and people dying?

"Let go!" she screamed at the top of her lungs.

"Give me that!" he yelled.

The leggings-float deflated in her hand.

"*Kau babi!*" she shrieked, pushing his body with her feet and twisting her arm, "You pig!"

She tore her arm loose and sank deep under the water. Her only hope was that she was a better swimmer than he was, and that in the darkness he couldn't find her if she swam away. She held her breath and swam deep and far—as far as her lungs would take her.

While she was under she could not hear the people or the splashing, and she could not feel the surface waves. It was strangely calm. She could feel only the pressure of the water all around her body and the larger movement of the ocean swells. For a minute she was free of the complex world above: free of the suffering and the fighting, free of the fear that someone else could take away what she was struggling so hard to keep.

Here, away from the madness on the surface, she knew that she was truly alone. It was her mind, her body, her life; only she could keep these things safe. In the end, she was the person who would save her if she were going to survive; no one could do it for her. She kept swimming underwater, though she needed air.

Where were the sharks? They were busy, if they were there at all. She could not think about them—not until she had to. From now on, she vowed to herself, she would deal with problems only as they presented themselves, one small step at a time; otherwise she would make herself sick with worry. So what if there were sharks?

She surfaced and drew a huge breath of air. The man was gone. She turned around to where she thought the raft was. It was gone, too, and in its place she saw shadows of heads bobbing, arms flailing, and bodies floating. The wailing and screaming had resumed, as had the violent shadows of men fighting men—or sharks attacking men. She could not hear or see Catherine or Richard, but according to her new pact with herself, she was not going to worry about their fate, or anyone's fate, until she was safe.

"Please let them be O.K.," she whispered.

Then she turned away. There was nothing for her here. The people—the bodies—would attract sharks all night, and she was too afraid to stay near the other desperate passengers. She would swim for shore and hope to intercept the rescue boats along the way.

13

In the darkness Emily could not see the island of Weh or the rugged coast of Sumatra. The moonlight was bright, but not bright enough to illuminate anything in the distance. Instead the moon cast a bluish glow in a wide path from itself to Emily. It was only enough light to see her watch and the glimmer of waves, only enough light for her to feel the expanse of empty ocean without any indication that it would end. Still, she knew the land was there somewhere — she had seen it clearly from the upper deck of the ferry — and that when it became morning again, she would see both Sumatra and Weh.

She twirled in a circle, slowly surveying the horizon. The swells lifted her in their peaks and lowered her in their troughs, so that she could get a good view only for a few seconds at a time. In the peaks she saw a light—a solitary speck of light from land far away. How far and which shore it was she didn't care. The ferry had sunk somewhere between Sumatra and Weh, so it had to be one of those, hadn't it? It had sunk after it had traveled an hour or more, so she had to be far fewer than eighteen miles away from either coast, hadn't she? It might be ten miles at most.

She knew she could swim at least two miles without resting—that was about 140 laps in a twenty-five-yard pool. Multiply that by five . . . it would be very hard, especially in choppy water, but not impossible. Not impossible. Thank God the water was so warm; she knew that cool water was dangerous after a time, even for a good swimmer.

She tied the deflated leggings to her camisole strap in the front, like an ugly black corsage. The silly leggings. They were nearly all that she had right now. In her mind, her life had begun in that locker, and she had been born into her new world with very little—an undershirt, a watch, a pair of underpants, and leggings. Like a newborn baby born into poverty. But unlike an infant, who for years knows nothing about what luxuries the world can offer and innocently accepts what little is provided, she knew that plentiful food and home and comfort were rightfully hers, and that she didn't have them. It was a cruel knowledge. She ached for her parents. She ached for everything that she normally had, for what she had come to think would always be hers.

She settled into a breaststroke. She tried to keep up a good pace—not so fast that it was tiring, but not so slow that she got nowhere in the swells, which were strong. Sometimes she dipped her head under with a few strokes, tucking her chin to her chest in proper breaststroke form to loosen her neck muscles, but mostly she kept her head erect and her eyes focused on the distant light that was guiding her. Better to swim with her head up, declaring her allegiance to the surface. Her entire world came to this, she thought: if she stayed above water she would live.

When she did put her face in the water she could feel the ocean all around her: an enormous, undulating nothingness around her small body—a black nothingness that wanted to swallow her.

"No, it's not nothingness at all," Emily said out loud about the ocean. "It's worse than that. It's the opposite of nothingness." It was an entire world of its own, teeming with life. A world in which humans were unfit, poorly evolved, and laughably out of place. She knew the surface of the earth was two-thirds water, and at that moment she felt like she was drifting in the middle of those two-thirds, swimming without fins and without gills. She was an oxygen-dependent mammal, a hairless, gangly ape plopped into an environment that had every advantage over her.

"Stop it, Emily," she said out loud.

It was nice to hear her voice. Almost like talking to someone real.

"You'll drag yourself down with bad thoughts . . ."

So what was a good thought in this situation?

"Yeah, what's good?" she said.

"Here's something good: you know how to swim," she answered herself. She took a few strokes, then laughed out loud. "That's really pitiful! Is that all you can think of? 'You know how to swim!' That's like saying, 'You're not dead.'"

Well, it was true, come to think of it. She wasn't dead. And that was a good thing. That was maybe the best thing of all. The worst case would be death.

"Maybe not," she said thoughtfully. "Maybe suffering would be worse. And I'm not suffering, not really." Yes, things could be worse.

She stopped and peered at her watch, waiting for her eyes to adjust to the light. It was midnight. Not even close to dawn.

She wanted to sleep. She had never stayed up all night. The closest she had come to staying awake all night was the plane trip from the States to Malaysia a year and a half ago. She had found it hard to sleep on the plane, even though she knew she should, to try to get a jump on the time change. When they landed, her mother had said, it would be morning in Malaysia, and they would have to take a smaller plane to Medan and then a bus to Banda Aceh. It would be a long day. So Emily had spent several hours with her eyes closed, restlessly adjusting herself in her seat, trying unsuccessfully to sleep. The more she had tried, the more agitated she had become that she wasn't sleeping, until it was hopeless.

"It's because I hated the idea of coming to Southeast Asia. I hated leaving home. That's why I couldn't sleep," Emily said out loud to the silent ocean. "I was angry and I couldn't sleep."

Now, nearly two years later, she must still be angry, she realized. If she had ever come to terms with it, she wouldn't have gotten on that ferry and she wouldn't be here, in the ocean, this very minute.

She remembered her first week in Banda Aceh and frowned. She put her face in the water and stretched her arms out in front of her as far as they would go, as if she could reach into the memory and brush it away with the tips of her fingers. She blew out big, slow bubbles from her mouth and felt them burst along the skin of her neck and down the inside of her camisole as she glided through the water.

The first thing she had noticed when she got to Banda Aceh was how hot she was all the time. Not the kind of hot that she enjoyed in the summer outside Boston, when the air smelled of baking pine needles and she played until the sweat trickled down around her eyebrows to sting the outer corners of her eyes. On those summer days she felt alive and glistening—barefoot and barely dressed in shorts over a bathing suit—like a native girl exploring her tribe's territory. When she tired of the heat, she would fling herself onto the lawn under the cool sprinkler and get rained on in the bright sun. Or she would retreat to the shade of the woods at the end of the street to pick wild blueberries.

No, on Sumatra the heat was wet and crushing and inescapable. It made her feel as if she were a walking, rotting corpse. There was no better way to describe it. It was something that she became accustomed to, slowly, but at first it sucked away her energy. The moistness enveloped her and seeped into every crevice of her body: between her legs, under her armpits. Cornstarch and powder provided only temporary relief. When she was caught in a tropical downpour—which seemed to happen almost every day—the steam rose off her drenched body and clothes as if she were an enormous block of dry ice evaporating into the thick air around her.

She had turned thirteen soon after she had arrived. On her birthday she had noticed red patches on her chest. It wasn't like the prickly heat that she got whenever she neglected to use her cornstarch. These patches were inflamed, itchy little spirals. It was ringworm. She cried inconsolably. Worms, under her skin! "It's prehistoric here! It's Third World!"

"It's not worms," her father said. "That's an unfortunate misnomer because of the way the skin lesion is shaped. It's a fungal infection. We can take care of it with a simple antifungal cream."

"Lesion! Skin lesions!" she wailed. "A fungus is a mushroom! Humans shouldn't live in climates where mushrooms grow in your skin!"

Her parents had chuckled together at that outburst. At the time she had thought, was this really funny to them? That their baby was being infected in this godforsaken sweatbox? She remembered how a burning balloon of anger had swelled inside her stomach and chest, how she had stormed into her makeshift bedroom, with a fiery urge to slam a door that wasn't there. Instead, the balloon of fire in her chest burst open, and flames licked up her neck and head, and she fell facedown on her bed and sobbed until dusk. Then, drained and pale with a raw throat and swollen eyelids, she sat down to her birthday supper.

Emily's eyes focused on the horizon again. She had been swimming off course and was no longer headed toward the light. She shook her head and blinked. She was tired and daydreaming too much. She'd have to put some effort into staying awake, into concentrating on the task at hand, without allowing the whole desperate situation to get to her. She had to follow that light.

Emily's arms were tired. She turned onto her back and sculled with her hands down by her side. The swells were smaller now. The moon had a fuzzy aura around it, as if she were looking at it through smeared glass. It was not quite full and so it had an imperfect, oblong shape. It seemed to stare down at her like a head, cocked slightly to the side.

She gazed at the sky. There were fewer stars now, too.

"It must be getting cloudy," she said.

It was too dark to see the clouds until they were close to the moon, then they would pass quickly in front of it and blink her into darkness for a moment.

"Well, I hope there aren't too many," she said to the sky.

"I don't think I could live without you, moon. It feels good to have you looking down on me. I know you're looking down on my parents right now, too. Maybe they're looking up at you, and it's kind of a link between us."

For some silly reason she suddenly had a picture of Luke Skywalker calling telepathically to Princess Leia while he was hanging from the chute on the bottom of the city in the clouds. She squinted her eyes at the moon, and in her head she said, Olivia, James, I'm here. I'm here.

She sighed. If only she had that kind of magic.

She straightened up to check for the speck of light on the horizon. She didn't want to get off track. Then she lay back and sculled some more, looking at the sky. Now a real cloud, a thick one, was passing slowly in front of the moon. She held her breath as the sky grew dark; it happened gradually, as if the moon were on a dimmer switch. The blue glow around her became smaller and smaller, until she was floating in the center of a weak spot of blue light, and then finally in full blackness. She straightened up again and treaded water. It was dark without that moon. Very dark.

She let out her air and drew a little gasp more. How long would it take for the cloud to pass? She peered out into the darkness. She swallowed. She took another little gasp of air.

"This is stupid," she squeaked. She cleared her throat.

"You're not really afraid of the dark, are you, Emily?" she said in a bigger, deeper voice. She began swimming the breaststroke again.

In the dark she was alone. She couldn't even see her own hands trembling in front of her. She didn't like not having her body as company; she needed to see her arms reaching in front of her. Those arms proved with each stroke that she was here, alive.

"I still have my voice," she said, defiantly. And the sound of the water, she thought.

She strained to hear the waves and she heard something in the distance. Was it a motor? She held her breath and stopped swimming, staying as silent as possible. Her heart was beating hard. It could be rescue boats. It could be a commercial ship. It could be another ferry.

She listened, and sometimes she thought she heard a hum. But it would fade into nothing, and she would be left with the sound of the water licking against her body, and the sound of her breath, short and shallow. Was that something she saw out of the corner of her eye? She spun around. Nothing.

"I'm hallucinating," she concluded. "I'm so desperate for those boats, I'm making them up in my mind. This is just like seeing a mirage in the desert."

She found the light on the horizon and started her breaststroke again. The blue glow of the moon began to reappear around her, steady as a nightlight in a child's bedroom. To her relief she caught sight of her hands again, and her arms, keeping her company, spreading in front of her in a steady rhythm. She looked at her bracelet. She had forgotten about that.

"Well, I guess I don't just have leggings and a watch," she said. "I have a bracelet, too."

Her father had brought it to her from Kota Gadang. He had gone to the village to vaccinate children and he always brought something back for her. Usually it was something little, something locally made and fun. This time it was even more special, more beautiful.

It was silver, made of delicate, spider-web strands that were twisted around each other. At irregular intervals there were purple amethyst beads anchored in the strands. To Emily, they looked randomly placed, as if the spider had left the carcasses of its last meals dotted along the bracelet. It was beautiful. And it was digging into her arm. The motion of swimming against the swells and waves repeatedly pressed the sharp clasp against her wrist, and for the first time that night she realized that it was cutting her.

She tried to change its position on her wrist. She turned it so the clasp faced up. She pushed it lower toward her hand to loosen it and get it off her arm. It rode back to the same spot and gouged at the tiny wound with each stroke.

There was nothing worse than a small, neglected cut in the tropical heat of Indonesia, Emily knew. The temperature and humidity were just right to breed bacteria; ordinary splinters, blisters, or even scratched mosquito bites could become quickly infected. She had gotten used to tending to wounds right away, keeping them as clean and as dry as possible and applying antibiotic ointment to everything. And what happened if you soaked a wound for hours in the salt water of the ocean, she wondered?

"You have to get rid of this bracelet," she said out loud.

"I can't get rid of it! James gave it to me," she answered herself.

"You don't need it; it's not helping you. Why don't you just let it go?"

"Well," she shot back, "you really like that bracelet. That's something you want to keep."

"You really plan on living, don't you?" she said.

Yes, she did, she decided. And she could live without

the bracelet. She stopped swimming and treaded water.

"I'll make James buy me a new one," she said finally, opening the clasp and letting the bracelet drop through the water to the bottom of the ocean. "That's it. When I see him today, I'll tell him he has to buy me a new one."

15

It was one-twenty. Just four more hours or so and it would begin to be light again. Emily was anxious to see land, to see her goal, and to keep a lookout for the rescue boats. It was so typical of Indonesia that there were no boats yet, wasn't it? Someone in an office somewhere was making the decision — slowly, importantly — while she was swimming, blundering in the dark toward land she couldn't see. This puffed-up official was probably at that moment considering whether it was too dark, or whether the seas were too rough, which of course they weren't. Or maybe the boats were out there already, but looking in the wrong place.

"The wrong bloody place," Emily said, thinking of how Richard would say it. He'd find some way to laugh about it, to make a joke of it and take the edge off her nervousness.

"I wish you guys were here," she said to Richard and Catherine, wherever they were.

She put her lips in the water and blew out to make bubbles, the way she did as a six-year-old when she had been learning to put her face in the water. She had been in the Minnow League on the YMCA swimming team. She hated swim practice. She'd hated swim meets. The pool was so cold that she had had to work up her courage just to get in it, and the coach—his name was The Coach as far as she ever knew—had been a former Olympic swimmer who had never won any medals.

"Hey, Slake," he would say, loud enough for everyone to hear. "Are you a rock or a fish?"

"A fish, Coach," she would reply dutifully, though she felt like a rock.

"What kind of fish, Slake?"

"A minnow."

"So get in there and swim like a minnow!"

Under the scrutiny of her teammates, she'd have no choice but to jump into the frigid water and swim, like a rock masquerading as a fish.

She blew some more bubbles. The warm water felt surprisingly smooth and soft on her lips. She wished she could drink it. She was thirsty, and was probably getting dehydrated with all this swimming. When was the last time she'd had a drink? It was on the dock, she remembered. She'd had enough money for an avocado drink called *es alpukat*—one of her favorites and a safe thing to buy off a cart if you were afraid of food poisoning. It was made with coffee essence, palm sugar, and condensed milk. It was delicious and sweet.

Emily wished she had some now. But caffeine was probably not the right thing to drink when she was dehydrated.

"Lemonade, maybe, really icy," she said out loud. "No, just cold water, in a frosty plastic bottle. Yeah, and tons of plain rice, some vegetables, and a big fat *Baronang* fish." What was she thinking? Not fish! Not while she was dragging herself through an ocean!

"Meat," she said with satisfaction. "Meat*loaf*. Mashed potatoes. Peas. Chocolate milk. Mmm. Now you're cooking, Emily."

She stopped to tread water. She untied her leggings from her camisole strap and blew them up. Then she looked at her watch. One forty-five. She yawned, a huge, lung-cleanser of a yawn. An alarming yawn, because it reminded her how tired she was. Could people ever get so tired that they would fall asleep while swimming? Would her brain quickly wake her up to stop her from drowning if she accidentally nodded off?

"I've had enough," she said. Then she looked up into the sky. The stars were twinkling. She closed her eyes. She had never prayed before. Each time she had been in a church it was as a tourist, admiring the architecture and religious art with her parents from a purely historical point of view.

"Dear God, can you help me? I shouldn't have run away. Why didn't I just go home and cry? Yes, I was stupid, so is this my punishment?" If so, it seemed harsh, she decided. Are most people's gods harsh or loving, she wondered?

"Do you hear me, God? If you're there, and you're listening, I've had enough. Was there some point you were trying to make with all this? Is it a *Wonderful Life* kind of thing? Because if it is, I . . . you know . . . I get the point."

She started to swim again, holding the inflated leggings. What was it Jimmy Stewart had said at the end of that movie when he was tired of seeing what the world would have been like if he — well, if his character, George Bailey — hadn't been born? And what were all those awful things that had happened in the world without George Bailey? This is good trivia to keep my mind going, Emily thought.

O.K. Without George, the town had been taken over by Old Potter. And Potter had changed the town's name to Pottersville. Shoot, what was the name before that? Let's see, it was Fall something. No! Bedford Falls. That's it. And George's wife had become a spinster, and his beautiful old house had decayed, and his four cute kids had never been born. Oh yes, and without George there to save him, his brother had died as a child, and the transport of soldiers his brother had saved during the war had died, and his uncle had gone into a nut house.

What were George's kids' names? One was Zuzu, because she had given him the rose petals. Zuzu's petals. The others were . . . Tommy, and Petey, and . . . ? A girl. Can't remember. And so anyway, there was George on a bridge, in the snow, with his wet hair falling into his face, whispering the lesson he had learned from seeing that terrible outcome of a world without George Bailey.

"I want to live again. I want to live again," Emily said out loud, quoting George Bailey on the bridge.

She sighed, a long deep sigh. What *was* the oldest girl's name in the movie? She was playing "Hark the Herald Angels Sing" over and over again on the piano, practicing for a recital. And George yelled at her by name. . . . What was that name?

"Janie!" Emily blurted out loud. That's it! Janie, she thought. In the movie George yelled, "Haven't you learned that silly tune yet? You keep playing the same thing over and over . . ." and then Janie cried because her dad was angry at her.

Emily heard faint crying floating around her like mist hanging over a pond. Was she imagining it?

"I'm losing my mind," she said, shaking her head to clear the sound.

But it was real. There was crying somewhere near her. She stopped and listened intently. It was coming from her left, but from far away.

She began to swim, quietly, in the direction of the sound. It became louder so slowly that she had to concentrate to keep on track. After a few minutes of swimming, in the dim blue light ahead of her she began to see a dark blob, a sobbing blob of something. As she approached, she saw by the shape of the shadow that it was a small person.

She swam closer. It was a child.

A few more strokes. It was a boy.

Now she was near him. It was *the* boy, *her* boy.

It was the waif she had shoved into a life vest on the ferry.

16

The boy was crying so hard that he hadn't noticed Emily approach. His dark, thin hands gripped the orange life vest tightly near his collarbones. His face was bent down, and his nose nearly touched the water with each quivering sob. His hair was a spiky, jumbled mess.

"*Selamat pagi,*" Emily said in a quiet greeting. The boy nearly jumped as he looked up, wide-eyed.

"Get away from me!" he shouted in Bahasa Indonesia. Then he took his right hand off the vest to splash at her, while his legs kicked frantically underwater, as if he were trying to run away.

"Go away! Go away! *Go away!*" he shrieked, splashing her in the face and running harder.

"Stop!" Emily said in his language as she turned her face away and shut her eyes against the water. "I will not hurt you! I will not hurt you!"

"You can't have my floaty!" he screamed, using an Indonesian word Emily had never heard before. But he stopped splashing and put his hand back on the vest. He was still running, twirling around as he did because of the way he was kicking, his hair bouncing up and down with the motion.

"What? Pardon me?" Emily said, confused. It was almost funny the way he was twirling and bouncing. She started to follow him.

"That evil man tried to steal my floaty, and Allah sent a *shark* for him! Do you want a shark to eat you? If you come near me, a shark will get you, I swear it! So you'd better stay away from me or else!"

Emily suddenly understood. The floaty was his life vest.

"I will not take your — your floaty, I promise," Emily said. Oh God, she thought, had he really witnessed a shark attack up close?

He looked at her out of the corner of his eye. He stopped running and kicked more gently under the water. He stifled a sob.

"Yes, you will. You want my floaty."

"I do not want your floaty. I cannot lie, I would like to have *a* floaty, but I do not want *your* floaty. I want you to have it. I think I can swim better than you can swim, and so you need it more."

She searched his black eyes. "Please believe me."

He looked into her eyes for a long while, then he stopped kicking. His eyelids were swollen and sagging. The muscles in his body became loose. His face became expressionless. He was falling asleep with his eyes open. It happened quickly and silently. His grip loosened on the life vest, and his head began to sink, leaving the life vest floating above him. Emily splashed toward him, but before she could get there his nose touched the water, and he awoke with a start. He squirmed spastically, his hands tightening their grip again, pulling him up and into the vest. He choked and started to cry.

"Oh no!" Emily said. Well, that answered her question about falling asleep in the water, she thought.

"I keep sinking out of my floaty!" he lamented. "I keep sinking into the water!"

"It is because you are not wearing it right," Emily said, remembering her moment with him on the ferry. She reached for him, and he pushed his feet into her stomach, but it didn't hurt.

"Don't touch me!" he said.

"There is a . . ." She didn't know the Indonesian word for "strap," and she couldn't remember the word for "rope."

"There is a thing," she went on, "that is not—put together . . . underneath your legs. It will keep your floaty tight."

He looked at her suspiciously.

She said, "Will you let me help you?"

He watched her for a moment. He looked down at his own hands gripping the vest and then back up at her.

"You can help me." Then he blurted, "But remember the shark!"

She said steadily, "I remember."

She swam behind him and found the strap dangling. She held it firmly, treading water, and turned his body sideways to find the buckle in the front. She let her leggings-float deflate and held it in her mouth to free up her left hand.

"I will put it under your legs now," she warned him, talking through her teeth.

She pushed the strap between his legs and brought it near the buckle in the front. It took her a minute to thread the strap, because she had to stick the webbing through metal slits that she couldn't see well in the moonlight. Her legs were cramping from kicking to hold up her weight while her hands were busy with the strap. Finally it was attached correctly, and she pulled the strap up while she pushed the shoulder down with the other hand. As she did, his body went up and the life vest rode down until it was snug.

"Aie!" he said, as if he were hurt.

It wasn't a perfect fit—he was such a puny thing— but it was much better.

"There," she said, taking the leggings out of her mouth. She was relieved to be able to scull again with her hands.

He was silent. She blew up her leggings-float, watching him.

"What's that?" he asked sullenly.

"These are my pants," Emily said, "I must use them as—as my floaty, because I do not have a real floaty."

She saw his eyes dart toward the water where her legs would be beneath her, then look quickly away. It was too dark for him to see her legs under the water right now, she knew. In the daylight, he would probably have seen them, distorted slightly by the waves, long and white, and it would surely have been the first time he had ever seen so much pale leg in his young life.

"How old are you?" she asked.

"I'm nine years old. How old are you?" he mumbled.

"I am fourteen years old. My name is Emily, and you?"

"Isman."

"Good morning, Isman, I am happy to meet you," she said politely.

"How can you be happy right now?" he said.

"I am happy to talk to someone," Emily answered honestly. "I have been lonely. You must be lonely, too."

"I've been hungry, and thirsty, and sleepy," he said firmly.

"Me, too," Emily said quietly. "But I think most of all I have been lonely." Then she added, "And scared."

"I'm not scared," he said, too quickly. "I've only been worried that someone will take my floaty." His voice became small. "I don't know how to swim well."

"You will be fine," she said. "The boats will come to get us, and everything will be good."

"Will the boats come?" he asked earnestly.

"Yes," Emily answered, gripping her leggings-float tightly underwater. Was it a lie?

"Will they save *Ibuku,* my mother? And my father and brother, too?"

She hesitated. "I do not know," she said truthfully. "I hope so."

"But while we wait for the boats," she went on, "I think we should swim. We should try to swim to land. Do you not think so?"

"I've been kicking toward that light," Isman said, pointing with his thumb to Emily's speck of light.

"That is where I have been swimming as well," Emily said.

Isman started to say something, but instead he cleared his throat.

"What . . . what is your name again?" he said finally.

"Emily," she said.

"Ehm-lay," he said in a whisper, testing her name.

"Em-i-lee," she said.

"Ehm-*lee*," he said, loudly. "Shall we . . . shall I swim with you, Ehm-lee?"

"Yes, Isman," Emily said, "I would like to swim with you."

I t was slow going, with Isman along. When they first set off together, he kept his hands on the life vest near his collarbones. His bony legs and small feet were poorly suited to propulsion underwater.

"You do not have to hold your floaty with your hands anymore," Emily told him. "It is tight enough that you can swim with your arms."

He thought about this for a while. Then he loosened his grip a little to test her theory, and when he was satisfied that she was right, he took his hands off altogether. When he found that he wasn't slipping through the vest anymore, he began to use his arms to swim. His stroke was a choppy dog paddle, in which he slapped his arms down on the water with his fingers spread wide. It was next to useless. They would get nowhere at this rate.

"Here," Emily said, "let me show you." She swam in front of him and turned to face him.

"First, you must try to lie on your belly as much as possible when you swim. If you are standing up, like this," she straightened her back, "you will mostly stay in one place after all your work."

"I don't want my face to go in the water!" he said angrily.

"Your face does not go in the water; you just lie more — more flat, like this," she demonstrated. "Try it."

Isman stretched his neck out like a goose, as if his body would follow. He kicked his legs madly until his chest dipped in the water, trailing behind his long neck. He arched his back and his legs thrashed, spraying water in all directions. He stopped kicking and bobbed back upright.

"The floaty makes me stand up!" Isman wailed.

"Yes, so you have to try hard, and think hard, to keep yourself on your belly." Emily continued her lesson. "Number two, your feet. You must kick your feet behind you like a pair of scissors." She wiggled her index finger and middle finger on the water's surface like tiny kicking legs. "Try to keep them under the water but . . . but still very near to the air, do you understand?"

"You're not a good teacher," Isman said.

"Number three, your arms. If you do this," she did the dog paddle with her arms, "you must keep your arms and hands under the water all the time, and push the water . . . like you are reaching forward for — for a sack of rice with each hand and then pushing it under you. Push the water as if you are pushing it all to your feet. And close your fingers." She held up her cupped hand.

Isman frowned as he listened.

"If you want to try another way with your arms, you can do this." Emily did the breaststroke with her arms. "That is, reach your arms out to the side gently. Try it!"

Isman stretched his skinny neck into the goose position again, kicked his legs hard to get prone, and pushed his arms to the side in a kind of breaststroke. Instead of long, flowing pulls, he began the stroke with his arms already open, by his sides, so that it was a stumpy, inefficient motion. Emily swam alongside him.

"Reach your arms out in *front* of you, then pull to the side," she instructed. "In *front*, then side—yes!—in *front*, then side. . . ." Suddenly she cried, "Keep your feet underwater!" when she noticed his legs splashing again.

Isman yowled defiantly at this outburst. He switched his arms to a dog paddle, first a slapping one, and then—either because she had told him not to splash or because he disliked the spray that he was causing to his own face—a smoother one with his arms under the water and his hands cupped. His neck was still stretched out like a goose.

"You're a bad teacher!" he yelled. "I'm more tired than ever! I hate this way of swimming! I hate you!" He stopped swimming altogether and began to cry.

He was trembling, and Emily realized abruptly that he was too tired to learn. He was so small, and so young. She shook her head. He had been through so much already. How tired must he be, at two o'clock in the morning? His bedtime was probably five hours ago or more. Here she was, five years older and much stronger, and she had been through more than she could bear.

"*Ma'af*," she said softly, "you are right, I do not know how to teach well." He didn't look up, but he stopped crying and sniffed.

"I have an idea for something different," she said.

"I don't like your ideas, Ehm-lee," Isman said to the water. He yawned, and moaned as he let out the air. A shiver went up his back, like a cat.

"But this is a good idea," Emily said. "I think you should sleep for a time, and I will watch you to see that you are safe. You need to sleep, and now that I am here, you can sleep."

He looked up, with the faintest glimmer of hope in his eyes. Then, as if a bucket had been poured over his head, the look washed away, leaving a gray, sagging face in its place.

"How can I sleep without falling into the water? How will we get anywhere if I sleep?" The tears welled up again. "And I'm so tired. It's not fair. Don't talk of sleep!"

"No, no, do not cry, Isman," Emily said. "My idea is that I will swim and pull you while you sleep." She held up her leggings-float, with her eyebrows raised.

"That's your floaty. What good is it?" he asked bitterly.

"Well, it is not a very good floaty, but it will be a good . . ." Darn, she thought, how do you say "rope"? ". . . a good thing to pull you," she said finally.

She pointed with her thumb to his life vest. "Your floaty holds you well now. You can turn to face the sky, on your back. There is a . . ."

Strap, she thought in English.

". . . thing," she went on in Bahasa Indonesia, "that I can tie my pants to on the back of your floaty." She reached behind him and put her fingers through a loop of webbing by the neck.

"See? I will tie the pants to this thing and I will swim while you sleep on your back. It will be good!"

The glimmer of hope returned to his hollow eyes.

"Why would you do this?" he asked.

"Because I want to sleep, too," Emily said. Then she realized that her answer made no sense. She thought for a second.

"But I cannot sleep," she said, "so it will give me pleasure to see you sleep."

He looked at her skeptically. Then he looked up at the moon as if to consult someone else and took a deep breath.

"O.K.," he said, turning around to make the loop accessible.

"I'm closing my eyes now," he announced.

She smiled, and as she knotted the end of one pant leg through the loop, he whispered the words she had heard near the raft, *La ilaha illa Muhammad Rasul Allah.* She felt his body relax, and he was immediately, soundly asleep.

"And when you wake up," she said quietly in English, "I hope you'll be a little refreshed and a lot more cooperative."

She tied the end of the other pant leg to her right ankle. She glanced one last time at her watch. It was twenty minutes after two as she set off for the speck of light, with her new baggage in tow.

18

Right away, Emily missed Isman's company. Finding him had energized her. And she liked speaking in a foreign language, because it distracted her from everything else. Now, in the moonlight, with the quiet sound of the ocean around her, she was aware again that she was exhausted. She was working harder than ever, only to make slow progress.

In spite of his small size, Isman was heavy to pull, because of the friction of his body against the water and the fact that he was a dangling, dead weight. She could only kick her right leg gently, so as not to pull him under with each stroke, or cause his body to roll from side to side, and so her arms and left leg bore almost the entire burden. If she wanted to make reasonable progress she had to pull hard. And the only stroke available to her, aside from the crawl, was the breaststroke. Her shoulder muscles were not up to the task.

"I'll be sore tomorrow," she said out loud.

"There you go again," she replied cynically. "You assume there will be a tomorrow."

There had to be. There had to be a dry tomorrow, a tomorrow in which she and Isman walked on land and slept in beds. A tomorrow in which they ate warm food and drank as much as they wanted.

Isman began snoring behind her, and she found the sound comforting. She concentrated on swimming rhythmically, so they could get somewhere and also to mark time. If she swam at a pace of about one mile an hour—an ambitious but reasonable goal if the currents were favorable, she thought—she and Isman would have traveled four more miles by dawn. Actually, they had probably already traveled several miles, through a combination of swimming and drifting, before they met each other.

They might be very close to the light, closer than they thought. The sun might come up later and there, right in front of them, would rise the misty moorings and harbor of Banda Aceh or Weh. Wouldn't that be a nice sight— mangrove trees along the shore, with their roots arcing in and out of the water like a woven basket? Come to think of it, wouldn't daylight be encouraging? After all, they weren't really out in the middle of nowhere, as the darkness suggested. They were between islands that were quite close to each other.

Emily thought about sunrise. As light began to filter over the ocean, the world would slowly become a black and gray field of dull water. Then, as the sun was close to peeking over the horizon, the dim outlines of the islands of Sumatra and Weh would appear, and the water would start to glisten. Finally, the full sun would illuminate the details of the islands—the volcanic mountains, the lush greenery, the swaths of geometrically planted fields, the roads and houses—so that she and Isman could judge distances well. There might be the sight of boats far off, circling around, searching for them. The world would become alive. Emily and Isman would be alive in that world. They would make it to land and into the arms of their families.

Emily pulled and breathed, pulled and breathed. For an hour or so her mind was almost empty, her thoughts suspended by the perpetual motion, the feel of the water, the rhythm of her lungs. She was there to pull and to breathe.

Slowly she became aware of a slight chafing along the inside of her arms, where they rubbed her chest, and it drew her out of her meditation. She decided to try the crawl stroke for a while, to keep her arms from rubbing that spot and developing sores. The salt water was not soft after all, as it had first seemed. It was abrasive, like extremely fine sandpaper.

Emily thought about Isman's family. Who *would* be there for him on shore? He had mentioned a mother, father, and brother. Were they floating out here some-where, too? If they had died . . . oh, how horrible—would he be an orphan? She straightened up with alarm.

"Wait a minute," she said. "That's useless worry." She shook her head. "Not allowed."

She put her face under and continued the crawl. But she couldn't shake the image of his family. She was actually lucky, wasn't she, that she had been alone on the boat?

She knew her parents were out there somewhere, on land, and that she just had to find her way back to them. They were safe. They were alive. She was alive. There was so much hope for her in this situation, really.

She thought suddenly about the woman who had drowned, the woman she promised herself she would not think about. What if that woman was Isman's mother? No. What an awful thought. The odds were small—next to nothing—with all those hundreds of people on the boat. That woman was probably a stranger to Isman. Yes, almost surely a stranger.

But she wasn't a stranger to somebody in the world, Emily's mind said, jumping ahead of her so that she couldn't catch up with it to rein it in. That woman was somebody's daughter. Maybe somebody's sister, or mother. Emily swallowed. She began the breaststroke again, so she could be above water.

"Stop," she said to herself.

But she couldn't stop her mind. She was too tired, it was too dark, she was too hungry, she was too thirsty, she had been swimming too long, and she had seen too much. She was not strong enough at this moment to stop her mind. It wandered of its own accord, showing her pictures, creating images and sounds that looked real, that flashed before her like a slide show of her subconscious.

First there was Isman, playing a game of bottle caps in the dirt road. Then there was the woman, calling to Emily. Next the woman appeared standing over the crumpled, wet bodies of a boy and a man. She was reaching to the heavens, and then she was collapsing onto the bodies. She was sobbing; the kind of sobbing that comes from the deepest loss, where a part of the person's soul seems to spill out with each cry. Her mouth was open, and her face was contorted with pain. She looked up at Emily, searching for someone, anyone, who could make the world right again.

Suddenly Emily understood why the woman had allowed herself to drown. And that perhaps she was wrong about the woman. Is it possible that sometimes death is an answer?

"No, never," Emily said, but uncertainly.

Her eyes filled with hot tears. Still, she would not cry. Not yet. Not while she was dragging Isman. The boy snuffled and let out a soft whine in his sleep, as if he were having a bad dream.

Poor Isman, she thought. So small, sleeping in an oversized life vest, entrusting his life to a teenage stranger. Oh, Isman. He was fighting with all his might to get back to a world that might be destroyed for him.

"Stop thinking about that," Emily commanded. She would tackle one thing at a time, she reminded herself, and the current task was to swim.

And so she swam. She swam until she was sick of swimming and wanted nothing more than to simply stop swimming, but she pressed on. She swam the crawl longer than she could imagine anyone had swum the crawl. But of course that wasn't true. There were people who greased themselves up with Vaseline and swam across the English Channel, just for fun. Fools. She switched to the breaststroke for a while, then the crawl, and then the breaststroke again.

It no longer felt like night. The sky was somehow different than it had been an hour before, as if it were preparing itself for sunlight. The moon was lower and there were fewer stars, but it was more than that. Emily thought, it's like watching a caterpillar in a cocoon: you can't quite say what's different, but a change is taking place inside.

19

Emily looked at her watch. It was four-fifty. She had been towing Isman for more than two and a half hours.

"My, my," she said sarcastically. "Where *does* the time go?"

Isman snuffled behind her. He awoke with a start. Without warning he began to thrash, as if he were tumbling through the air, trying to catch himself, trying to break his fall. The more he splashed, the more startled he seemed by all the water that was hitting him. He mewled, and then coughed with little barks because of the water in his throat.

Emily's leg jerked this way and that because it was still attached to his vest by way of the leggings. She wanted to turn to face him. She flipped over onto her back so she could see him better. He was facing the other way.

"Isman!" she cried. *"Isman!"*

He stretched his goose neck up at the sound of his name, but he was confused.

"Wake up, Isman! Please!"

He stopped splashing and looked around until he saw her. He blinked hard, and then stared in a stupor at Emily. Slowly, something in his eyes became aglow again.

"Ehm-lee," he said simply, disappointedly, after he regained his consciousness.

He had twirled around to see her, wrapping the leggings around himself as he did, shortening the distance between them. He frowned at the leggings and at her foot, which was almost touching him, assessing the situation slowly in his mind.

"We are tied together," Emily said. "If you turn around again, I will untie us."

Still moving sluggishly, Isman twirled around, more dutifully than before his nap, perhaps because he was still sleepy.

"La ilaha illa Muhammad Rasul Allah," he murmured quietly.

Now with more length to work with, Emily was able to lift up her leg and untie the one pant leg. Then she untied the other pant leg from the loop of webbing on his vest.

"I want to sleep more," he said in a monotone to the expanse of the sea.

"Can you not stay awake, now that it is almost morning?" she said to him. She was glad to be talking again.

"How long did I sleep?" Isman asked, as she spun him around to face her.

"Only two and a half hours," Emily replied. "But you must think about how, when the sun comes again, we will be able to see Sumatra and Weh. That will make us happy. That will wake us up!"

Isman's eyes brightened as the flame of optimism leapt from her and began to kindle something inside him.

"I want to see Sumatra!" he said. "When . . . when will the sun rise?"

"I think in one hour, but will it not become a little more light before then?"

"Yes!" he said, now enthusiastic. "Yes, it gets light even before the sun peeks over the horizon!" He paused, and a mist passed over the new flame in his eyes, dampening it down to just a smoldering glow.

"Do you think we're close to land?" he said, now quietly.

"I do not know," Emily answered. "But if we are not, the boats will see us in the light of the day."

"The boats," Isman said.

She understood the look on his face. Where were the boats? Why had she and Isman spent the whole night in the water without hearing or seeing boats?

"We will swim now," Emily said. "This way."

Isman furrowed his eyebrows and bit his lip, and Emily could tell that he was concentrating.

"In the name of Allah, Most Merciful, Most Gracious," he said softly. His face cleared, and with great deliberation he stretched his neck and kicked his legs in a little splashing scissors kick until he was swimming prone. Then he put his hands together as if he were praying, and pushed them out straight in front of him, with great care. Finally he pulled them out to the sides and down, in a smooth breaststroke motion, his chin well out of the water and nose high in the air.

Emily grinned. "That is wonderful, Isman. Wonderful. Soon I will teach you to kick like a frog."

"A frog," Isman laughed. "You're funny, Ehm-lee."

Emily blew up her leggings-float and swam next to him. Almost immediately she noticed something small and round bobbing in their path. At first she thought it might be a child's plastic ball, but as they approached she saw that it was a tomato. A tomato! Food!

Two thoughts immediately bombarded her, and the first was not very charitable: if Isman were still asleep, the tomato would be all hers. She had swum for both of them, hadn't she? She was the one who hadn't eaten since breakfast, now almost twenty-four hours ago, right? She shook her head. That wasn't fair; she had no idea how long it had been since Isman had eaten. And he was so small for a nine-year-old. All the swimming and struggling had probably burned up the last of whatever meager fat reserve his body had.

The second thought ricocheted in the background as her brain wrestled with the ethics of who should eat the tomato: rather than a human offering food to the gods, the gods were sending the human a tiny offering. Hats off to you, the God of the Sea was saying to her, you've fought well so far and herewith I give you a token of my admiration.

"A tomato!" Isman said suddenly, with great excitement.

Emily smiled. Slow boy, she thought.

"Who gets it?" Isman said quickly, before they reached it.

Emily got there first. She plucked it out of the water and in a short moment had fondled it all around in one hand. It was smooth and very red, even in the funny light of a fading moon. It was ripe and round and plump. It was easily the most beautiful thing she had seen in her whole life.

"We both do," Emily said. Then she handed it to him.

"Here," she said, as he eagerly reached for the prize, "you eat half of it, and then pass the rest to me."

He looked at the tomato and said, "Thanks to Allah, al-Barr, al-Wahhab, al-Razzaq."

Emily watched him eat, aching for her half.

"I know who Allah is," she said, "but who are the others?"

Isman laughed, covering his mouth with his hand. "Him! Those are his names, too. There's only one God, Allah. But he has ninety-nine beautiful names." He licked the juice dripping down his wrist. "Each name tells something about Allah: al-Barr means the Source of All Goodness; al-Wahhab means the Bestower; al-Razzaq means the All-Provider."

"Ah," Emily nodded, watching another drop of juice fall into the water, wasted.

Isman held up the bitten tomato. "This is from Allah. No matter who grew it or who bought it, Allah alone made this tomato possible. I try to remember whatever I have—whatever I love—comes from God. Saying the ninety-nine names helps remind me."

He took a last measured bite and handed Emily the rest.

"My father says that nothing belongs to us in this world, Ehm-lee. This is why we share our good fortune with others, and give alms to the poor. This is what we learn: that everything is on loan from God."

After she ate her half of the tomato, Emily sucked on her fingers, as if to absorb whatever molecules of nutrients might be stuck between the cells of her skin. The most wonderful thing about the tomato was how juicy it was, how it was almost like having a small drink and meal at the same time.

They set off toward the speck of light. Isman grunted lightly as he worked.

"I'm going to eat another tomato when I get home," he said.

"I am going to eat ten," Emily answered, and Isman laughed.

"Can I tell you a secret, Ehm-lee?" Isman said. Then he went on, sheepishly, "I never liked tomatoes."

Emily smiled. "You ate my half, then," she said.

"But I loved that tomato," Isman said. "I honestly loved it. I know now that I was wrong about tomatoes."

They swam some more in silence. Emily looked up. The stars were gone. The sky was becoming grainy with the promise of morning. She looked at her watch.

"It is half past five," she said.

"Oh!" Isman said. "I should say dawn prayers."

"Can you pray as you swim?" Emily said, remembering that Muslims prayed on their knees, and prostrate, and standing, but she didn't know the order, or if it was even required to assume those positions.

"I could try to do some of the prayers, if we stop a while," he said. "Would you mind?"

"Will it take long?" she said. Then she wrinkled her nose, "Oh, *Ma'af!* I am not polite. You have to pray, do you not?"

"If I can, I should make *salaht* five times a day. But I should also face Mecca while I pray, and I don't know exactly where that is." He looked around him, deciding. "The sun rises in the east, and the horizon seems brighter over there . . ." he murmured.

"It's good, I think," he said at last. "I trust that Allah is All Forgiving."

"What is *that* beautiful name?" Emily smiled.

"Al-Rahim, al-Ghaffar, al-Afu . . ." Isman listed.

"You are good!"

"I also have to wash first, to be purified before I pray." He lifted a hand, cupped and full of water, then let the water drain through his thin fingers. He looked over at her. "It shouldn't be a problem."

Emily laughed. He could be wry. She moved away a few strokes to give him privacy, but watched from the side.

First he closed his eyes. He became loose in his vest and sank a bit inside it. For a moment Emily wondered if he had fallen asleep. When he opened his eyes he whispered, "In the name of Allah, Most Gracious, Most Merciful." He rubbed his hands all over, as if he were washing at the sink, being sure to get in between his fingers and up to the wrists. Then he scooped some water with his right hand, sucked a little into his mouth, swished it around, and spat it out. He scooped more water with his right hand, raised it to his nose, and sniffed some in, then snorted a bit and rubbed his nose with his left-hand fingers. He washed his face, from top to bottom and from ear to ear. He washed his forearms, starting with the right. Next, using his right hand, he wiped his head from his forehead to the nape of his neck and back again. He rubbed with his index fingers inside his ears, while stroking the backs of his ears with his wet thumbs. He wiped his neck with both hands. Then he strained to lift his feet, one at a time and right foot first, to scrub them.

"Oh, Allah," he said quietly, "make me among those who are penitent and make me among those who are purified." Then he began to pray.

Emily examined him. His hair was clumped together in drying mats. It was so sun-bleached that some patches looked dull in color. The strands clinging to the nape of his neck were dark and wet. He had a sloppy haircut. Perhaps his *ibu* cuts his hair, Emily mused. His skin was the color of a creamy cup of coffee. His nose was broad and flat. With his long neck sticking out, and the big vest bulging from his back above the surface, he looked something like a large turtle bobbing on the ocean.

Isman's prayers were in Arabic, not in Bahasa Indonesia. Emily heard the words "Allah Akhbar" many times. Other than that she recognized only the word "Muhammad." The prayers seemed to repeat, and were nearly melodious in their rhythm. Isman didn't attempt to change positions, but she could see he used his hands wherever possible. Praying came easily to him, in the same way that Emily dressed herself in the morning — layering familiar, warm clothes on a body that she had memorized.

Emily assumed her resting position while she waited, with her legs dangling and her head back, keeping her lungs full and taking only short, shallow breaths. She was eager to start swimming again to stay warm. Her jellyfish stings itched. The skin on her legs felt tight, as if it might split open.

The eerie blue glow of the moon was gone and the simple, accurate light of dawn slowly filtered everywhere in its place. Emily sighed with relief, and heard her own sigh whoosh in her ears. There is something mysterious about nighttime that makes a tired person hallucinate, that makes a frightened person more scared, that makes a logical person lose perspective on the world. Even a very sleep-deprived person can think more clearly when it's dawn. She watched Isman in the dim light; the rhythm of his motions and words lulled her.

He finished his prayers.

"I'm looking, but I can't see land," Isman said.

Emily focused on the light they were following. It was still just a beacon, with no island attached.

"No, I cannot see land either. But there is more light every minute. We have waited so long. The land will show itself soon."

"When it does we'll know where we are and how far we've come," Isman said.

"Yes."

As she stared ahead Emily saw something—the shadow of a large lump of something—in the distance. It seemed wavier that far out for some reason, and the lump lolled in and out of the waves. It looked like a person. No, it had no independent movement; it looked like the dead body of a person.

It was a body, she was almost sure of it. There was no point in waiting to figure it out; they had to go around it. Emily couldn't bear to see it up close.

"Here, turn around," Emily said suddenly. She grabbed Isman by the back of the vest and turned him in the direction opposite the speck of light. Then she began pushing him lightly, her heart thumping.

"Why?" Isman said. "What are you doing, Ehm-lee?"

"I think there is a . . . a person there."

He looked over his shoulder, but Emily was in the way.

"Alive?" he asked.

"No."

"Let me see," he said.

"No! I cannot go past it. We will go this way," she said, steering him to the left. They could bypass it and then get back on course later.

"But I have to see," Isman said. "Stop pushing me, Ehm-lee!"

"Why? Why must you see? If it is dead I do not want to see it!" She choked. Her throat felt hot and swollen.

He said steadily, "I *have* to see, Ehm-lee, because of my family."

Emily let go of his vest. His family. He turned and looked in her eyes. For a moment she saw the world in them.

"You don't have to come," he said quietly. "You can wait here, and I'll swim back to you."

She knew she should go with him, but she couldn't. Her body felt like lead. It was all she could do to keep her head above water and breathe. Isman was already on his way. He swam the dog paddle, lumbering at a steady pace, with a strength she couldn't muster. Emily concentrated on breathing and on looking at the speck of light, to keep her mind and eyes off the lump that she was sure was a body.

Isman returned a few minutes later.

"It's a man; it's not my father," he said flatly. His face was gray.

"I am glad that it was not your father."

Isman hung in his life vest without moving. He stared down at the water. Emily waited quietly.

"I don't want to sound like a baby, but I want *Ibuku*. I want my mother," he said.

"I know. You are not a baby."

Emily looked in the direction of the body and decided they might be far enough to the side to swim around it. They resumed their course toward the light. She chewed the inside of her cheek. Who was the body, she wondered? Why was it this far out? Had the person made it this far, only to drown? Would they encounter more bodies on their way to the light? Had they passed people in the night and just not seen them?

The morning was becoming noticeably lighter. The speck of light now appeared to be at the top of a small, hazy island. A few minutes passed, and the island didn't rise up before them, as Emily had expected when she believed it was Sumatra or Weh. In fact, they were only a few miles away at the most, and it was much too small to be either. But it was land.

She peered to the left and in the distance saw the lump again, less shadowed and more clearly a body this close. She held her breath. Isman wasn't looking in that direction. He was looking at the island.

"Ehm-lee!" he said. "There's the land we're swimming for. I can almost see all of it."

"Yes," Emily said.

"It's small," Isman said. "Very small."

"It cannot be Sumatra or Weh," Emily agreed. "I thought it would be one of those two."

"Oh, Ehm-lee," he said. "There are more than seventeen thousand islands in all of Indonesia. Why didn't we think it might be something other than Sumatra and Weh? This one probably has only a name and one light, to warn ships away from the shore."

"We must still swim there," Emily said, "because it is close. I feel I can swim no longer. I am so tired, and I need . . . I need so much to sleep. I just want to sleep."

She was suddenly overcome by lethargy. Here was the daylight she had been living for, and what had it given her? A dead body, a tiny, uninhabited island, and no boats in sight. Would they simply become stranded on an island after all this, to die of dehydration within hours?

"From the frying pan into the fire," Emily said to herself in English.

"Pardon me?" said Isman in Bahasa Indonesia.

Now it was almost six o'clock, and the sun they had waited for edged up on the horizon. As it did the layout became instantly, perfectly clear. The sun rose in the east.

The little island in front of them seemed to be the first in a series of four small islands stretching in a row to the north. To their left—south—would be Sumatra; to their right and behind them—north-northeast—would be Weh. But neither was there. Why couldn't they see Sumatra or Weh?

Peering at their little island, Emily saw the last glimmer of the speck of light, almost overcome by the morning sun. The light appeared to come from the top of a light-house, though only the lantern showed. The base of the tower was blocked by land and water. All at once Emily realized that, in the expanse of the ocean, the curvature of the earth limited the distance that a swimmer could see along the surface of the water. She had seen only the highest hills of Weh from the top deck of the ferry, but of course she—she and Isman and all the other passengers—would not have seen either Sumatra or Weh while they were in the water.

Oh, majestic, populated Sumatra and gorgeous Weh, both with food and drink . . . and beds. Wasn't it just their luck that they had instead been swimming all night toward an insignificant nothing of an island?

Emily looked again to her left, and to her horror the body was nearly upon them.

"It's the man," cried Isman. "Ehm-lee! Why is he moving so fast?"

The body was carried in a strong current. It had been swept toward them in a loop, clockwise, without them seeing it. In a second Emily realized that the loop was part of an enormous whirlpool, and that they were being carried into it as well. There was no time to think. She grabbed hold of the webbing on the back of Isman's vest as they became caught up in the swirling water.

They were carried just ahead of the body, which was gaining on them. Now Emily could see that it was floating facedown, slightly bloated with gases and barely covered in tattered clothing.

"He's touching me!" Isman wailed. "Get him away! Get him away!" he screamed over the sound of the waves. He was kicking at the body and pushing it with his arms.

Emily still had a hold of his vest. She and Isman must not become separated. She could feel that the current was strong enough to pull him under. The dead body was instantly irrelevant.

"Leave it!" she commanded, choking on water that rushed into her mouth.

"Swim, Isman! Swim now!"

21

Emily didn't know anything about whirlpools. This one was large in diameter, and the current was strong. They were spinning in huge circles with the body.

After a few minutes of struggling, Emily realized that all their effort in swimming was only keeping them from being sucked into the rough center, but was not enough to break them free of the whirlpool. They were wasting precious energy and making no progress.

With one hand still on Isman's vest loop, she abandoned the leggings-float to free the other hand for swimming. Somehow she would have to drag both of them, side-stroke, out of the whirlpool, but she didn't know how. If only Isman were a better swimmer, they might have a chance of saving themselves individually. How could she possibly fight for them both?

Eventually the dead man became stuck in the center of the whirlpool, spinning around like a leaf at the bottom of a drain. Periodically he was sucked all the way under, only to bob back up and be sucked under again. Sometimes he stayed down longer than Emily thought she could hold her breath. She felt the hairs rise on the back of her neck and on her arms.

Isman was crying. He was limp and crying and totally useless.

"Kick!" she ordered, breathlessly. "Kick with me! I will pull you, and you will kick!"

He continued to cry, but he kicked dutifully underwater. In that way they stayed away from the center, but they were still not able to break free.

Emily tried attacking the edges of the whirlpool from every direction, almost systematically, as if she were following the spokes of a wheel. On each spoke, she pushed hard toward the outer circle, trying to find its weak point. Every time she thought they would make it through, the edge seemed to grow, or move away from them—or maybe it wasn't really where she thought it was—and slowly they would start circling again, clearly still inside the swirling currents. Over and over as they approached what she thought was the edge, she would scream, *"Now!"* and they would make a special, strong effort to break free. Each time, battered by exhaustion, out of breath, and fighting cramps in her arms and legs, almost but never quite there, she would give up, and they would swing back into the clutches of the whirlpool.

Emily got to know the whirlpool well. There were other objects living in it with her and Isman and the dead man, objects that seemed to be from the boat: bags and shoes and even a small door. It took a long time to get to know all the objects. Like ducks diving under a lake to forage and then reappearing in a different spot, an object would pop into view where there had been nothing before but the swirling surface of the water. Then it would spend some time in the center, turning rapidly, until the eye of the whirlpool sucked it under again, only to spit it out at some later time. Together these objects were doomed to travel in eternal circles. Eventually nothing new appeared, and Emily realized that she was slowly dying in the whirlpool.

Her right hand was red and raw from holding on to the loop of webbing on Isman's vest. Could she still hold on if it cut into her hand? No, she didn't think so. But if she didn't hold on, he'd be carried in toward the bloated body and other debris in the center of the whirlpool, and together he and the corpse would spin around and around and eventually be sucked under. Oh, God. He'd be scared and alone and dying just outside her reach. He would try to hold his breath, knowing that he couldn't, feeling what it was like to drown.

Emily let out a muffled cry. They were so close to that damned island, and yet the whirlpool was defeating them! She had no energy left. How could anyone expect them to have enough reserve to tackle this—this insurmountable obstacle, after all they had been through? And what kind of sick joke was it to spin a dead person in their faces as their lives drained from them with each revolution?

There must be a way out. But what was it?

She knew about rip currents near the shore in Massachusetts. She had never been caught in one, but James had told her what to do. She should never fight to swim toward the beach, he'd said. She should swim to the side, parallel to the shore, at an easy pace until she bypassed the section that had the rip current and was free to swim in to the beach. Above all, he said, think and relax.

But this was not a rip current—how could his advice help now? If she let herself relax, she and Isman would be sucked into the center like the other dead debris. Swimming with all her might against the current was just barely keeping them out of the eye of the whirlpool. How could she relax?

Think and relax, she said to herself. Think and relax.

Obviously fighting was not working, just as it didn't work to fight the rip current. What was the analogy to swimming along the side of the beach? The only direction she hadn't tried was swimming *with* the current, in the same direction as the swirling waters. But wouldn't this just hasten their trip to the middle, to the deadly eye? Or would it allow them to break free, by swinging out and away? Maybe it was possible to swim with the current, while making their way gradually to the outer limits, until they were truly at the edge and out of the whirlpool's clutch.

It was the only thing left to try. She would collapse soon from exhaustion. Isman had stopped kicking and dangled as if he were already dead—she had to try something.

"Kick with me!" she yelled to Isman.

He startled as if he had been asleep. Then he let out a frightened moan as it became clear that they were headed in the direction of the current. But he kicked as he was told.

Emily pulled hard with her left arm and dragged him with her right. The first thing that happened was that they began to move fast. Too fast. The current was swifter than she realized, and swimming with it made them travel even faster. She knew she could never control this amount of speed. Isman was nearly on top of her now. He was lighter than she was—would he ride right over her and hold her under?

Think and relax.

Emily concentrated on working toward the outside. Ignore the speed, she said to herself. Swim hard with the current and to the outside. The sidestroke was fine for this, she assured herself. Pull to the outside. She went under for a moment and lost her bearing. The water rushed around her ears, welcoming her under the surface, embracing her. She choked, and water rushed up her nose, burning her raw sinuses and the back of her throat. When she came to the surface she and Isman were closer to the eye than they had ever been. The door hit her in the head as it spun for its turn down the enormous drain. She was failing.

Think and relax.

"Kick again!" she cried to Isman.

This time, rather than swimming hard with the current, she let it carry them at its pace, and worked only on inching toward the outside with each revolution. One inch at a time is good enough, she soothed herself. Try for one inch. She developed a rhythm. Like running a marathon, she reasoned, the less she flailed when she was the most tired, the less energy she would expend. Don't try for more than an inch. Be happy with an inch on each revolution.

Somehow, instinctively, Isman picked up her rhythm and kicked in time with her pulls.

"*La ilaha illa Muhammad Rasul Allah,*" Isman grunted, over and over, in time with his kicking.

With the new rhythm came slow progress, and progress brought calm to the swimmers. With the calm came a surer rhythm until there they were, near the edge of the whirlpool.

Another inch, they were at the edge.

Another inch, they were free.

For a time they couldn't stop the rhythm. They pulled and kicked, pulled and kicked, leaving the whirlpool behind them until the rhythm had ebbed out of them. They stopped and turned around. The dead man, a shoe, and the door were spinning around and around. But Emily and Isman were free.

Emily lifted her left arm out of the water. It was quivering from overwork. She looked at her watch. It was seven-twenty. They had been in the whirlpool for more than an hour.

22

Emily was flooded with feelings of release, of collapse, and of grief. She began to cry. She had promised herself she wouldn't, but she couldn't stop herself. She was too tired not to cry.

"Ehm-lee!" Isman said with alarm. "What's wrong, Ehm-lee? Are you hurt?"

He put his hand on her shoulder. She shook her head, but pulled away because the weight of his hand was enough to push her underwater.

"We made it, Ehm-lee!" he said, out of breath. "You should be happy!"

"No, we are dead, Isman. We are dead," she sobbed.

"You're wrong, Ehm-lee," he said as if she were merely misinformed. "We're alive."

Her face dipped under to the nose, and Isman tried to lift her chin. His touch was so soft, so tender that it took her by surprise. She stopped crying.

"I am tired of living, but not living," she said weakly. "I am tired of swimming. I have not stopped swimming, I have not rested, for . . . for too long. I am only a child!" She began to cry again.

"You may be a child, but you're also grownup." He thought for a moment, still breathing hard. "When you see something is necessary, you do it."

Emily sniffed.

"One time my mother drove me in my Aunt Halijah's car," Isman said. "The tire got a hole in it. Ibuku had never changed a tire before—we don't even own a car— but she got the book out, and the tools, and she changed the tire." For a moment Isman's eyes had a faraway look.

"I'll tell you a secret," he said finally. "When you swam to me in the water last night—so white, so big, so . . . strange—" His eyes scurried over her features as if he were seeing her for the first time again. He paused for a long time on her green-gray eyes. "It took me a long time to get used to you."

Emily grunted. "That is not a secret," she mumbled.

He went on, "Even so, right away I thought, 'This is the will of God, this is *takdir*, that this stranger is here. She'll help me go home. I accept God's plan for me.'"

He smiled weakly and said in a lower voice, "And now I'm not only used to you, but you're my friend. I still think Allah wants us to go home together. But I also want us to go home together."

Isman pointed a thin thumb in the direction behind her. "Look, Ehm-lee."

Emily turned around. The little island was hunkered down in the ocean, tiny and homely and solid, as if it were waiting patiently to be noticed, to do its job and rescue them. It was no more than a large rock, really, but only a couple of miles away at the most.

"We've come very far," Isman said quietly.

Emily stared at the island. What would the sand feel like on her knees as she crawled her way out of the ocean? How heavy would her body feel after so many hours of near weightlessness in the salt water? What would it be like to walk on the shore? How long would it take before she dried in the hot sun—what does it feel like to be dry? What does it feel like not to move a muscle, to sink into the sand, and, without any effort, let gravity hold you in place? What does it feel like to lie down and sleep?

"Will you take me there?" Isman asked. He raised his eyebrows expectantly.

"Yes," she said, taking a deep breath. "I will take you there."

So they set off for the island at a very slow pace. Isman dog-paddled, and Emily kicked on her back, sculling with her hands down by her sides. The sun was strong already, even this early in the morning. She was going to get burned, especially in the water, and as far as she could see, there wasn't a shade tree or overhang anywhere on that island. But that was useless worry, she reminded herself. She should think about something else.

"Isman?"

"Yes?"

"When we were back there in the—what is the word?—in the circles . . ."

"It's called a whirlpool. Yes?" He swayed a little from side to side as he paddled.

"What was that you were saying, again and again?"

"*La ilaha illa Muhammad Rasul Allah.* It's Arabic. It means, 'There is one God, Allah, and Muhammad is his Messenger.' They were the first words I heard when I was born. I want them to be the last words I say or hear when I die."

"It helped you to kick," Emily said.

"It helps me all the time."

Emily closed her eyes and sculled gently. She pretended that she was at Long Pond back home in Massachusetts. It was a Sunday morning, and no one was out. Just a fisherman sitting silent and still in his rowboat, waiting for a catch. And maybe an old-timer, out for her morning swim, gliding slowly in the soft green water, not even making a wake, barely exercising, and drinking in the peace of the world. Emily almost fell asleep.

"There's someone there," Isman said.

Emily said, "Mmm?"

Isman hissed, "There's someone in the water!" Emily straightened up.

"Dead?" She looked around.

"No, alive," Isman said, as Emily caught sight of the person.

What she saw first was yellow. A bright yellow dot. Then she made out the dark head above it. It was a man. Then she saw an orange life vest. The yellow was his shirt. The green floating in front of him was a cushion from the boat.

"His shirt is yellow," Emily said. She knew that color from the ferry. That was the yellow she saw before she fell into the locker. She shivered. This man had been next to her as the ferry submerged, she was almost sure of it. Maybe he had even fallen against her. Could he have pushed her? She had no way of knowing. But in the end he got a vest and a cushion, while she had been trapped inside a locker. How did God parcel these things out? How can one person have nothing and another have so much?

"So? His shirt is yellow," Isman said. "He's lucky. He'll be easy for the rescue boats to see. We need to go to him."

"No!" Emily said.

"Why not, Ehm-lee? Maybe he can help us."

"No one can help us but us, and the boats," Emily said.

The man waved. He had been on a path for the island but now he was making his way toward them.

"Good morning!" he called to them in Bahasa Indonesia. He was looking at Emily. She wondered if he recognized her or if she just looked foreign. She couldn't tell what he was thinking.

"Good morning!" Isman called back. The man looked away from Emily and at Isman.

"Good morning!" he called to Isman. "I'm glad to see someone!"

"Do not get close," Emily said under her breath to Isman.

"Why not?" Isman hissed. "He *has* a floaty. He has two! He won't take mine."

"Still, we must not get close," Emily insisted.

"We're near the island," Isman said. "We've all made it. He won't hurt us. Besides, I think you should have a floaty. He has two! You should have one. Don't you want one?"

"Quiet!" Emily said, afraid the man would hear. "Yes, of course I want a floaty. But I — I know it would just . . ." She couldn't finish.

What she knew was that there was a truce that each person had with the ocean, and that it had taken her, and Isman, and this strange man all night to figure out how to save themselves. And if the truce were somehow disturbed, it might mean war all over again, and she couldn't bear for anyone else to get hurt. There was no sense in that. There was no sense in dying this close to their little island.

Finally she said calmly, "This man is happy with his floaties. I am happy without one. We must not . . . we must not change that."

Isman nodded. He did understand after all.

"Can you speak Bahasa Indonesia?" the man yelled to her.

Emily said, "Yes, I can."

The man had a plastic bag on his cushion, resting like a king on its throne.

"I have candy," he said, holding up the bag to Isman. "Come here."

Isman looked at the bag of candy and then at Emily imploringly. Emily took a deep breath. She nodded.

"Be careful," she said.

Isman swam his little dog paddle toward the man. The man reached into the bag and stretched out his hand, holding a bar of candy wrapped in blue paper. Isman took the bar.

"Thank you," she heard him say politely. The man said something that Emily couldn't hear. Isman said something back. There was a pause between them, and the man had nothing more to offer. Emily held her breath. Isman looked back at Emily, then at the man. He was deciding something. What was it? Emily wanted to know. Eventually Isman turned to Emily with a broad smile—he had beautiful white teeth that she hadn't seen up until now—and held up the candy bar. He paddled back to Emily. She sighed with relief.

You're a funny person, Emily, said a voice in her head. *Were you worried he would leave you for the stranger with candy?*

23

The candy was a chocolate bar, already divided into two servings in the wrapper.

"One for me and one for you," said Isman, handing the small treasure to Emily.

Emily gobbled her half. It was dark chocolate with coconut inside. Isman watched her eat. He pondered his piece.

"How can you wait?" Emily asked him.

"Did you know it's the holy month of Ramadan?"

"Yes. Can you not eat chocolate?"

"I'm not supposed to eat anything during daylight hours. This is the first year I've fasted."

"Ah . . ."

"I could eat it after sunset . . ."

"No, Isman. Sunset is too far away. You must eat it now. You must eat it for strength. You can break the rule," Emily said impatiently.

Isman stared at the chocolate in his hand. It was starting to melt in his fingers.

"You are so small just as you are!" Emily was beside herself. "You fasted yesterday! You fasted last night when you should have been eating! That is enough . . . that is too much for one as small as you! You must eat it! Please!"

"I ate the tomato," Isman pointed out. "But that was before the sun rose, so it was O.K."

The chocolate shone wet in the sunlight.

"Wait, I'm thinking," Isman said, squeezing his eyes shut. Emily held her breath to keep from exploding. His face cleared, and he opened his eyes.

"This is a part of the Qur'an that I've memorized: *So let those of you, who are present at the month, fast it; and if any of you be sick, or if he be on a journey, then a number of other days; God desires ease for you and desires not hardship for you; and that you fulfill the number and magnify God that he has guided you, and haply you will be thankful.*" He smiled as he popped the candy bar into his mouth. "I told you — Allah is forgiving."

Emily laughed with relief, so hard that she sank to her mouth and choked on some water. Isman grinned at her with chocolate between his teeth. He carefully licked up the residue on his fingers until they were clean.

"Someday I'm going to memorize the entire Qur'an, like my father and his father before him," he said solemnly.

They left their wrapper floating on the water. The man and the bag of candy were just a yellow dot again, traveling in a current separate from Emily's and Isman's. She wondered if they would meet again.

It was eight-fifteen. They were easily more than a mile away from the island; she could tell by comparing it with the view across Long Pond, which was exactly half a mile.

"Now that we have eaten candy," Emily said, "we will swim like fish to that island."

"Then we'll rest, and the boats will find us," Isman agreed.

In a perfect world, Emily thought. No, she corrected herself, in a perfect world none of this ever would have happened.

The sun rose high as they paddled toward the island. Somehow Emily found a tiny reserve of energy. It may have been from the candy bar, or it may have been from finally having a reasonable goal. With each stroke she could tell they were getting closer to the island. She was no longer living in a hopeless world of water; she was making her way purposefully toward something that would help her. She had swum this distance nonstop at one or two horrible YMCA swim practices, and she knew she could do it. Isman had a life vest, so she knew that he could do it as well, as long as she stayed with him. Now it was just a matter of patience, of making their way one stroke at a time without getting anxious.

After several minutes Isman said, "Oh."

"What?"

"I missed the *wayang kulit* last night. We were going to buy tickets on Weh."

"Shadow puppets!" Emily said. "Do you know I have never been to see a show?"

"Really? You'd enjoy it, I know."

"Tell me."

"The room is dark There's gamelan music playing. You stay up late because it lasts for hours. You eat, and nap, and watch . . . and then eat some more. The *punakawan*, the clowns, are the best part," he said wistfully.

"Fun," she sighed.

"Fun," he agreed.

"Isman?"

"Yes?"

"When we get home, let us go together to the next *wayang kulit*," Emily said.

He smiled at her and nodded.

He began to hum absent-mindedly. Emily liked the aimless tune.

An hour later her cheeks and shoulders felt hot and tingly, the way they did when they began to burn. She knew the rest of her was also burning, but without symptom. If—when—she got indoors again she would swell up, bright pink and blistered. She might get sick. Even her sheets would be agony against her skin at night.

What a mixed blessing daylight is, she thought. I longed for the sun during the night, and now I'm getting first-degree burns and inducing skin cancer.

She tried not to think about it. There was nothing she could do. Right now her task was to swim.

The next time Emily checked her watch it was almost eleven o'clock, and it was as if she had never eaten the candy bar. Whatever energy it had given her was gone. Isman was no longer humming. He was wide-eyed, panting, and chapped. His lips were white and flaky around the outsides.

The island was growing in front of them. They were close enough that with each stroke she thought they were nearly there, but they never quite made it. Distances in the water were so difficult to judge, she realized. The more they swam, the closer they seemed to be, and yet they were still so far. It reminded her of the math teaser she had learned in fourth grade: if you repeatedly shortened the distance by half between you and any object, when would you reach the object? The answer, of course, was never. You could get right up to the object and there would always be an infinitesimal space that you could cut in half again.

But that problem must have something to do with the space between atoms, Emily thought. Is it really only a math problem? Isn't it also a physics problem? If there were no space between atoms, then you could reach the object, couldn't you? Atom would touch atom, and that would be the end of that. Are there spaces between atoms?

She was dizzy. She turned onto her back and closed her eyes. She shouldn't have been dwelling on math teasers; it was too tiring. With the sun near its peak — shining right through her lids as if they were made of pink rice paper — her eyes ached. She was still dizzy. Her eyeballs began to roll from side to side, uncontrollably. She tried to take deep breaths. She felt like she was spinning. She was spinning and she could not keep herself steady on the water.

She concentrated on the feeling of the water against the skin of her back to try to relocate herself, to try to make the connection again between her brain and her body. Her eyeballs were still rolling. She opened her eyes to focus on her feet. She could not do it, and she felt suddenly nauseated. She swallowed to hold it down. To hold what down, she thought? She had nothing in her to vomit.

Then gradually her eyes slowed their frantic pace and settled on her feet, still kicking underwater.

How frail her body was, she realized. She had always counted on its strength. She had always taken for granted that her body would be under her control. But the ocean was killing her, and there was nothing she could do to stop it. No, she couldn't count on living, the way she always had when she plummeted down ski slopes, when she forgot to wear her bike helmet, when she was slow to put on her seat belt. Life could be snatched away. The body is a fragile shell designed to hold the human brain. It won't always be here. It doesn't really belong to us.

I'm dehydrated, she thought. I'm getting too much sun and I'm dehydrated.

She turned back over to the front to continue the breaststroke. She needed more than ever to get to the rocky island.

Isman had gotten half a body length ahead of her. The island was so close. They were nearly there—this time it was true. They were so close that she could see every detail of its surface

It was dark in color, nearly black, with crevices everywhere. It was jagged and harsh. It was steep. Too steep to have a beach, she realized. It looked like the tip of a volcano poking above the water. They would have to climb on it and search for a flat area to rest. It actually looked sharp to the touch. It was wholly unsatisfactory. It was another joke in a series of cruelties. And it was all they had.

"We're there," Isman said. His voice was thin and reedy. Emily knew all at once that he had nothing left to give. He was at his limit. This lifeless rock, this substandard resting station, this slap in the face—it was the only thing that could save them now.

"You are doing so well," Emily said.

They continued the breaststroke and examined the island. They could see that the lighthouse tower was painted white and red, and it was clearly unmanned.

When they were no more than fifty yards away, the current became strong. It was pulling them to the right, to the northeast. The closer they got to the island, the stronger the current was.

It's because the island is so steep, Emily thought angrily. There is no beach; there is no coral reef; there is nothing to break up the current. The water barrels toward the island and then sweeps around it as if it were just an inconvenience, a minor detour.

"Ehm-lee!" Isman said desperately. The island was slipping away. They had swung around a small peninsula and were several yards past the end of the island now.

Emily looked back, and for a moment she couldn't believe what she saw. Richard was standing near the end of the island. His legs were bowed, as if under some great weight. He had a long, dirty rope in his hand, with something gray and round attached to it. And there was Catherine, lying next to him—dead?—wearing a bright orange life vest. It was not a hallucination.

"Emily!" Richard shrieked, catching sight of her. Catherine stirred.

"*Emily!*" he yelled even louder.

"*Richard!*" Emily shouted back.

Her heart was pounding. She reached her hand out to him as if she could somehow span the distance between them to touch him.

The ocean currents had pushed them all in the same direction, she realized suddenly. Richard, Catherine, Emily, and Isman, and even the man with the candy—all had blundered through the night in the same direction. The lighthouse had been a beacon, encouraging them to work with the currents, to strive for this island.

"Oh my God!" Richard suddenly looked down at his rope; he seemed flustered.

Emily looked back at Isman, whose eyes were wide. He was lighter than her and drifting faster to the north. The space between them was increasing.

Richard's hands shook violently, and his bowed legs looked as if they would snap as he tied the end of the rope to a sharp rock. Then he took the gray ball and threw it, pitifully, with two hands, toward Emily in the water. It didn't matter that he had no strength; the current immediately carried it in Emily's direction. The rope was surprisingly long. She started swimming against the current to meet it. The gray ball was a buoy—Richard must have found an old piece of a fisherman's net. Even luckier, somewhere in their journey they had found the life vest for Catherine.

"Swim, Isman!" Emily yelled over her shoulder, summoning new energy inside of her to reach her goal. Isman began to kick and splash, his eyes still wide, his mouth in a grimace.

Emily put her face in the water and swam the crawl. She swam as if she were at a swim meet. She swam as if it were the fifty-yard freestyle—a sprint so short that you were supposed to swim it "all out," using maximum energy for the whole event. Slowly, she got closer to the buoy. But the sprint turned out to be too long to sustain. Her maximum energy wasn't much, she realized. She lifted her head out of the water to breathe, her lungs aching with the enormous depth of the breaths she was taking, and began swimming the crawl with her head up.

The buoy and rope were almost within reach. She put her face in the water again, ignored her exploding lungs, and pushed one last time.

The rope was in her hands.

"I'll pull you!" Richard yelled to her, taking hold of his end of the rope.

Emily looked back for Isman.

He was too far away. He was swimming his little breaststroke hard, and losing more distance than he gained with each pull.

"Kick harder!" Emily screamed at him.

Richard tried to pull the rope, with Emily attached, against the strong current. He was too weak. Catherine got on her knees, as if she would stand and help, but then lay back down.

"Hold on!" Richard screamed to Emily.

"Swim harder!" Emily yelled to Isman.

It was no use. Isman had drifted so far that Emily could no longer make out his wide eyes on his face.

She looked back at Richard and Catherine on the island. With their light-colored shirts and Catherine's bright orange vest, they were sure to be seen if a boat came by. She looked at her hand, holding the rope. She looked at the long rope, a lifeline attached to a rock, with the buoy shivering in the middle. She looked back at Isman; he was so far away that she could no longer make out any features at all. He was vanishing as she watched.

She couldn't go home without him.

She waved hard at Richard and then pointed again and again in the direction of Isman, hoping he would understand.

Then she let go of the rope.

24

Emily swam for Isman. It was easy, following the current. She used the breaststroke so she could see where he was at all times. Richard called her name until his voice faded away to nothing. Isman let himself drift, waiting for her. She could hear him as she approached; he was moaning, "No . . . no . . . no," watching the rocky island recede into the distance.

Emily was equally stunned when she reached him. She had counted on that island for so long. In her mind it had saved them, and now it was gone. More than that, Richard and Catherine were on that island, and they were gone, too.

Because of the waves barreling against the island, the water had large swells on the lee side. Emily and Isman bobbed up with the peaks and then dropped down as if in a fast elevator—their hearts in their throats—before the onset of the next wave. Emily reached for Isman's hand. They would be separated if they didn't hold each other.

Emily surveyed the ocean from the peaks. There were still three islands near them, the sister islands to their lost island, stretching in a row to the north. The islands were no more than five hundred yards apart, but the water was rough around them, as if the ocean were angry at the repeated interruption.

"The other islands," Emily said, lifting her chin in the direction of the rocks ahead of them. "We must go to them!"

These islands were even less satisfactory than the first. They were smaller and just as jagged. The second was small enough that many of the swells crashed over the top. None of the islands would have beaches, she knew. They were probably all part of one volcanic peak, like the ridge of a mountain underwater, and these were the four highest points of the ridge. The current would sweep around each island, as it had around the first, picking up strength around the perimeter. The last ten yards of the swim—through this perimeter—would be the hardest. Oh God, would it be impossible?

Beyond the islands there was nothing. Emily knew that Thailand was out there to the northeast across the Strait of Malacca, and the Nicobar Islands were to the north-northwest, but both were hundreds of miles away. There would be no hope of rescue if they were washed from the Andaman Sea into the open Indian Ocean to the west. No rescue boats would search there, even if she and Isman could survive that long.

Emily pointed with her free hand to the left, to the west side of the second little island. Isman nodded his head. The current would sweep them alongside the island to the right, trying to suck them around the island and past it, so they must approach it well from the left, to give themselves plenty of room to fight the current. Emily noticed a wave pour over the top of the rock, and had an image of Isman being ripped off it, tumbling down its sharp slope and into the ocean. This island could be dangerous for them both. She decided that they would approach it, and if she judged it to be unsafe, they would go on to the next.

Getting nearer to the second island was almost easy at times because the current was so strong in that direction. Emily swam with her left arm, holding Isman's hand with her right. Isman kicked, with his head too high and the muscles in his neck stretched and taut. The sun was almost directly above, the heat pushing down on their heads as if it actually had weight.

When they began to feel the tug of the current dragging them to the right, Emily aimed them left, against the current. There they swam, seemingly in place, for an eternity. They were not losing ground and they were not gaining ground. The little island stayed about a pool-length— only twenty-five yards—out of reach. Emily could have thrown a stone farther.

Isman began to grunt. Minutes later the grunts became whimpers. Emily could feel the island slipping very slowly to the left—or rather, she and Isman were drifting gradually to the right. They were losing the battle.

All at once Emily hated the feeling of the water, all around her, touching every part of her. The island was solid and unmoving in the waves—so dry, so stable—if she could only pull herself onto it, crawl up it, she would be free of the water forever.

"Kick!" Emily demanded.

"I can't!" Isman cried breathlessly.

He let his legs dangle.

"Do not stop!" Emily screamed.

"I have to," he said.

The current picked them up and carried them away.

"I have to . . ."

Emily pulled frantically with her left arm. She dug her nails into Isman's wrist. She kicked wildly and pulled until her head went under and water rushed into her left ear, but it was no use. The second island was gone, already behind them.

"You idiot!" Emily yelled, when they had spun away and were bobbing in swells again. "You baby! You . . . you made us lose it!"

Isman squeezed his eyes shut.

Emily couldn't stop herself. A flood of heat rose up from her chest.

"You are killing us!" she said. "If I die, it will be because of you! Do you hear me? You are killing me! You baby! I hate you!"

While she was yelling, another part of her was watching him, watching this person who was totally defeated by the ocean and bobbing up and down with her. He was dehydrated and overexposed to the sun. He was covered in a white powder of sea salt. He was thin and drained. He had slept two and a half hours in the last day. He was empty and hopeless. And now he was being beaten by words. The part of her that was yelling couldn't stop. The part of her that was caressing him with her eyes hated the part of her that was yelling.

She started to cry, though her body was too dry now to produce real tears.

"I hate you," she said, to him and to herself, closing her eyes.

Isman cried quietly. They were still holding hands. They had never let go.

25

When Emily looked up, everything was exactly as it had been before. Isman was holding her hand, still shaking with quiet, dry sobs. The third island stood impassively in the swells. They were being carried in the current, and if they didn't swim for the island soon, they would miss this one too.

Emily waited. She was drained. She didn't want to move.

Isman's crying slowed, and then stopped altogether. After a minute, he looked up with red, hollow eyes, out over the waves. His face was expressionless.

But his hand was warm. Emily closed her eyes and felt only the warmth of his hand. It was the warmth of life. It was a body maintaining hope even when the mind had given up. Isman didn't know that his body hadn't

145

given up. Emily could feel his blood fighting to keep him warm. His heart would pump until the very end. His lungs would help him to breathe as long as there was air.

She opened her eyes.

"There is yet the third island," she said.

Isman said nothing. She couldn't blame him for being hurt.

He was still gazing through the waves, but his eyes were no longer empty. His eyebrows were furrowed.

"We will try again," Emily said gently.

Isman's eyes squinted now, as if he were nearsighted. Emily stared at him. He was looking at something. She followed his eyes out into the ocean.

At first she saw nothing. They were in the trough of a swell, surrounded by moving hills of water. Then when they rose in the peak she saw something, or she thought she saw something, but it was very tiny. They plummeted into another trough. Isman's gaze was fixed in place, as if the swells were not there.

"What is it?" Emily asked.

"A boat," said Isman.

"A boat?" she said, "Are you certain?" She searched through the swells and caught sight of something, very far in the distance. It did look like a boat, for that split second.

"It's crossing back and forth," Isman said. How could he see it better than she could? she wondered.

"Do they see us?" she asked. No, of course they don't, she thought. We're much too far away.

"No." Isman blinked and then looked at Emily. His eyelashes were stuck together, and they looked like black spikes.

"We must get their attention," Emily said, her heart beating fast.

They stopped holding hands and lifted themselves out of the water as far as they could, waving their arms back and forth.

"*Hey! Help! Hey!*" they shouted.

They sank into the water to their chins. It was no use. The boat was searching in the wrong place. They would look like ants flailing in the water miles away, even if the rescuers used binoculars and happened to look in the right direction. The waves and chop acted like small mirrors moving constantly in the glare of the hot sun. Everything looked the same as far as the eye could see: a blinking, glittering world of waves. The people on the boat wouldn't hear them, either; the water absorbed too much sound. The engine of the boat was loud. It was just too far.

"They can't see us," Isman said, looking to Emily for an answer.

"No, they cannot," Emily agreed.

But the boat was there! At least one rescue boat was there. Human beings were out there, milling around, looking for survivors. Finally they weren't alone; they were just invisible to their rescuers. All she and Isman had to do was to somehow become visible.

"We must go to the third island," Emily said suddenly.

"Yes," Isman understood. "There's a better chance that they'll see us on the island."

But as they turned to swim to it, the third island was gone. The current had already swept them away from it. They looked back to find it; the swells were rolling from the island toward them. There was no hope of swimming against the current to reach it.

"We must swim to the last island," Emily said. "We must not miss this one!"

They held hands. Emily pulled sidestroke with her left arm while Isman pulled with his right. Emily glanced at him as they set off. His face was gaunt. His eyes were sunken, so that you could see the orbital sockets of his skull. His lids were dark and shadowy. His facial muscle tone was weak, leaving him with an empty look. It was the look she had seen in the faces of dehydrated babies in her parents' clinic. She had helped to feed an electrolyte solution to the strongest baby, one painstaking spoonful at a time, a few spoonfuls an hour. By the end of the day the baby was alert, and smiling weakly, and her eyes had begun to have life again, but it wasn't until the next day that the ominous shadows around her lids were gone. Isman needed to be in a hospital, right now, drinking fluids and sleeping.

They were closing in on the last island. Beyond it Emily could see only ocean, grim, desolate, and welcoming.

Now the current was getting stronger, this time pushing them away from the island to the east. Emily felt Isman slow down. The swells were refusing them entry, and Isman did not have the strength to fight.

She was tired. She had fought the whirlpool and won, but since then she had lost to three islands and expended all that was left of her energy. She had given up the chance to be saved by Richard. She had been in the water for seventeen hours.

The island was so close. It wasn't fair that she couldn't get to it.

She looked behind her. In between the swells she could see the little boat. Were her eyes getting used to the distance, or was the boat getting bigger?

"Isman," she said, "the boat . . . the boat . . . is more near to us."

Isman tried to look back, but the vest rode up and blocked his vision over his shoulder. He stretched his neck and, with a groan, tried to look again.

"Keep swimming," Emily said, breathlessly. "I know that the boat is more near, I can see it."

The current was dragging them past the middle of the island now.

"You must swim more," Emily insisted. "This is what happened before!"

She swam as hard as she could. She kicked through cramping legs and pulled so hard that she dragged him, as if he weren't swimming at all. Still, it was not enough to make forward progress.

"Please!" she gasped in English, but she didn't know to whom.

Please, she said in her head. Please, let us on the island. I beg you, I beg you.

"I beg you!" she said out loud.

She heard Isman say, "Let me go! It's the will of Allah!"

They were nearly past the island now.

"No! Swim!" Emily commanded hoarsely.

"You have to let me go!" he yelled. "Then you can find me!"

"Isman!" she screamed, as he ripped his hand out of hers. He was instantly swept up in a swell and separated from her. She swam a frantic crawl stroke toward him, with her head above water and her hair splashing from side to side.

"No! Go to the island!" Isman yelled. Then she heard him shout, "Find me!"

She stopped and looked back at the island. She was at the western edge now, and Isman was past it, drifting toward the open ocean. Her mind raced. She looked quickly for the boat. It was still so far away, but distinctly larger. She had no doubt it was coming toward the little islands. If she were on the last island, the boat might see her. She could wave and scream until the boat found her. Isman was right, she could then direct the boat to rescue him. If she didn't get on the island, if she were swept away into the ocean with Isman, no one could tell the people on the boat where Isman was — or that Isman was, at all.

She swam for the island and away from her friend, bobbing alone on the surface of the harsh sea. It was the hardest thing she had ever done.

Emily put her head under and swam the crawl stroke toward the island. She took infrequent, gasping breaths to the side, choking on the waves. When she looked forward to see where the island was, she saw it slipping away. She was not going to make it.

She cried out in frustration. Instinctively, she took a deep breath and dove under. Immediately she sensed that the current was weaker underwater. It was her only hope. Using all her strength, with her lungs crushing inside her chest, she kicked huge frog kicks and pulled with big, sweeping breaststrokes as deep as she could toward the island. In the bright sun and clear water, she could see the island under the surface. She felt the pressure of the ocean pushing in on her from all sides.

She was getting closer to the island. Now it loomed in front of her with enormous black rocks and underwater plants swaying in the currents. The waves crashed above her onto the jagged shoreline, churning the water and sending fizzing bubbles deep under the surface. Now, rather than being drawn away from the island, the current lifted her roughly and tossed her onto her back underwater, sucking her in toward the rocks. She looked up and saw the sun through the crashing waves. She forced herself back on her stomach and swam up for the surface, but she was caught in a wave that was ready to break. It was too late. She was thrown against the rocks and into a crevice. She had time only for a quick breath before the next wave crashed on top of her, trying to drag her back into the ocean as it retreated.

Emily dug her hands into the rock, pulling off her index fingernail as she thrust it into a crack. She screamed in pain. Another wave pounded her and wrenched her feet from under her, forcing her chest and stomach against the rocks. She had to climb. She was being battered by the waves.

She crawled, one hand at a time, up the sharp rocks and out of the crevice. There was blood on her hand and both knees, and she could feel that she had other cuts, but she didn't have time to look. When she had dragged herself out of the crevice and out of the reach of the strongest waves, she crawled more slowly. Soon she stopped completely. With her head resting on her arms, her belly leaning against the incline of the island, and her knees propped on a rocky ledge, she fell asleep.

It wasn't real sleep, was it? Her brain was awake, flying outside her head, examining her from above — a rag doll draped on the dark rocks. If she were really sleeping, she wouldn't be aware that she was sleeping, and she would be dreaming. She was so weak. Perhaps what was actually happening was that she was bleeding to death.

She woke up and began to crawl again. She was so heavy that lifting her arms and legs was like lifting boulders. She trembled uncontrollably.

She climbed onto a jutting rock. It was big enough to sit down on. She leaned back against the rocks. She fell asleep again. This time she had a dream.

Isman was in his life jacket, spinning in a whirlpool. She was on a boat near the whirlpool. There was a captain on the boat who was looking through binoculars, over Isman's head, not seeing him. Emily tried to yell in her dream but nothing came out. She waved frantically, pointing to Isman. The captain didn't see her, even though she was right next to him. She shook his arm, but it was as if she weren't there. She jumped into the whirlpool and began spinning with Isman.

She woke up. She was dizzy. She felt as if she were falling off the rock. She looked up. There was a relatively flat area less than ten feet away; it was a good spot to stand and hail boats.

She had made such slow progress, and she had dozed so long, that she was completely dry. Her hair was like straw in front of her face, too stiff to brush aside. Her skin was on fire now, tender everywhere to the touch. How far must Isman have drifted while she slept? She had to stay awake; his life depended on it.

She couldn't stand up to climb; her legs were too weak, and she was having painful muscle spasms. Instead she pulled with her hands and pushed with her knees. Her mouth was parched and her tongue felt swollen in the back of her throat. When she took even a shallow breath, her lungs hurt.

She reached the flat area. She dragged her belly up onto the surface of it, then lifted one knee and pushed her whole body onto it, collapsing. She rolled over on her side, facing the ocean, to look for the boat, but she fell asleep.

In her dream she finally opened her eyes groggily, and the boat was close to the jagged island. Was it a dream this time or was it real? She lifted her head and called "Aaah," but she was so hoarse that nothing came out. She could see people on the boat. She pulled herself up, propped on one arm and waved, then she collapsed again. The rescuers seemed to be looking at her. They pulled the boat up near the island, and lowered a small rowboat. A man rowed it to the edge of the island, a big man. He leaped into the water with his shoes on. He climbed nearly effortlessly toward her, and her eyes rolled up into her head. She felt the shade of his large body blocking the sun. She heard his deep voice say in Bahasa Indonesia, "What a blessing you were so pale against the black rocks." She felt strong hands lifting her. Then something carried her down the steep hill — or maybe she drifted through the air — to the rowboat. Next she was on the deck of the larger boat. She was outside her body again, looking down on herself. She could see herself lying there, with her hair stuck to her face. She had on underwear and a torn undershirt and she was bruised and bloated. Her skin was no longer transparent, but a bright, angry pink all over.

She opened her eyes for a second and caught a glimpse of the man with the yellow shirt. He sat near her on the deck of the boat, sipping something steamy from a thermos. Catherine lay beyond him, asleep and disheveled. Emily's eyes rolled into her head. Somewhere behind her or above her—or in her mind?—a voice like Richard's said, "*And she walked away!*"

She heard herself moan, "Isman. Isman."

The big man said in English, "Who is Isman?"

"Isman," she heard her voice again. "With me. There. Please." In her mind she saw a picture of him, drifting west, deep into the Indian Ocean. She wanted to direct them to him, to be able to stand and point and say, "He's out there—you must find him!" but her eyes wouldn't open and her body was lead.

The voice that sounded like Richard said something. Emily heard only pieces.

". . . saw someone with her in . . ." Richard's voice faded away, and the big man said something in English about the direction of the ocean currents.

Emily tried to move. Something heavy held her down now, though she wanted to get up. She tried to lift the heavy thing off her. Floating voices said, "Rest. It's O.K."

"No, *Isman*," she heard her voice, only faintly this time.

"Rest . . . we know . . . just rest. We've radioed your parents. Can you hear? Emily, they're waiting; they're all waiting for you . . ."

Emily fell asleep. She didn't want to fall asleep. She dreamed she was waking herself up. Then she dreamed nothing for a very long time.

Later, the boat rocked gently in the swells. Emily stirred. She felt the hard deck beneath her, wonderfully solid.

She felt a blanket on top of her, soft and warm. It was the heavy thing that held her down, she realized. Just a blanket.

"Isman," she said weakly. Her voice was hoarse.

"Isman is here," said the voice of the big man.

"Can't you see him?" said Richard's voice. "We found him, thanks to you. We didn't give up."

She turned her head to the side and fought to open her eyes. Through the tiny bright cracks of her lids, like an overexposed photograph, she saw Isman lying next to her, wrapped in another blanket. His face was turned toward her, his neck and shoulders were limp, and he was watching her with his eyelids half open. She reached out to him. He found an opening in the blanket and slipped his hand into hers. He closed his eyes.

She rubbed the back of his hand with her thumb. His skin was thin and loose over the bones, like the hand of an old man, but still wonderfully warm, perseveringly warm.

She concentrated on how different it felt: her warm, dry skin against his. Finally dry.

What would this new dry world be like for Isman and for her when the boat docked? she wondered hazily. No, she shook her head slowly. That's not a thing we can work on now.

Her lids drooped unevenly, and her eyes rolled gently up. But she held his hand to make sure he'd stay, to make sure nothing took him away while she slept, because the next step was still to make sure they arrived together.

"Isman," she murmured, rejoicing in the word.

Author's Note

I wrote *Overboard* in part because of my own year and a half overseas as a child. I remember mourning the loss of my home and friends, the difficult adjustment, and the subsequent intense affection that I felt while I got to know and understand a new culture, people, and language.

I chose the setting of this book after reading news reports and seeing television interviews of a young American woman and a British couple who survived a ferry accident off the coast of Sumatra in January 1996. The American woman passed life vests to the other passengers as the ferry sank, neglecting to take one for herself. She swam alone for sixteen hours until Indonesian authorities rescued her—exhausted, sunburned, and dehydrated—from a small island.

No one knows exactly how many men, women, and children were on the ferry *Gurita* that day, but there were probably about four hundred. Of the forty survivors, three were women and one was a boy.